I0531470

ISBN: 0615941311

ISBN: 9780615941318

Library of Congress Control Number: 2013957982

Washington Academy of Sciences, Washington, DC

The Washington Academy of Sciences was incorporated in 1898 as an affiliation of eight Washington D.C. area scientific societies. The founders included Alexander Graham Bell and Samuel Langley, Secretary of the Smithsonian Institution. Then as now, the purpose of the new Academy is to encourage the advancement of science and "to conduct, endow, or assist investigation in any department of science."

Over the past decade the publishing industry has undergone dramatic changes. The old, proud publishing houses have, for the most part, become virtually indistinguishable from other commercial establishments, delegating their traditional editorial functions to agents whose primary purpose is to meet the demands of the market. Increasingly, authors are eschewing the agent-to-publisher-to-mass market route and are turning to on-demand, self- publishing. Whether the process includes a traditional publisher or not, editorial niceties and fact-checking often have no place in the process.

This has led to a number of problems, the worst of which is – from the Academy's point of view –the great increase in "junk science" being published both as fiction and non-fiction. The Academy therefore offers those Academy members who have written a science-heavy book, the opportunity to submit the book to our editors for review *of the science therein.* The manuscript receives the same rigorous scientific review that we accord articles published in our Journal. If the reviewer(s) determine(s) that the science is accurate, the author may then continue the publishing process of choice and the book may display the seal of The Washington Academy of Sciences. In cases where the Academy editors determine that the book is scientifically accurate but requires editing, they may return the manuscript to the author and request that it be satisfactorily edited.

A FINE CLIMATE for MURDER

a bea goode mystery

Peg Kay

Washington Academy of Sciences

ACKNOWLEDGMENTS

This book took a lot of reviewing. It had to be reviewed for accuracy in the wetlands, in the labs, in the oceans, in the woods and on the general subject of climate change. For those reviews, heartfelt thanks to Terrell Erickson, Chris Farley, Kevin Munroe, Jim Miller, Mary Jackson Clark and Barry Clark of Alpacas of Maryland, John Strickland, Shai Spetgang, and Drs. Mina Izadjoo, Mark Holland, and Gene Williams.

Dr. Vary Coates did yeoman (yeoperson?) editorial duty.

And finally, thanks to our redactor and friend Molly Cameron – you'll meet her namesake in the pages of the book.

Cover design by Emily Smith

NOTE: A Yiddish English Glossary precedes the Epilogue.

Characters in Order of Their Appearance

Dr. Bea Goode - The Great Detective and part of the management team at the U.S. Laboratory for Industry and Trade (LIT)

Dr. Alex Carfil - The Great Detective's husband and Director of the Computer Sciences Center at LIT.

Gertrude - an adolescent alpaca

Joe - a deputy sheriff

Don Cromarty - a member of LIT's management team

Lenore - secretary to the Director of LIT

Dr. P.I. Lee aka Pie - Director of LIT

Ben Goldfarb - a half-member of Bea's staff (shared with Don)

Jeanne Cameron - a member of Bea's staff

Marge Dunn - a member of Bea's staff

Jim Daly - a member of Bea's staff

Dr. Billy Norman - fisheries expert and a Department of Trade and Industry (DoTI) member of the committee

Dr. Julia Han - silviculturist and DoTI member of the committee

Dexter Hamilton - manager of Cabot House

G.Douglas Mapledent - botanist and Department of Rural Affairs (DRA) member of the committee

Dr. Ronald Drumm - soil scientist and DRA member of the committee

Howard Farrington - agronomist and DRA member of the committee

Chrissie Daly - Jim Daly's college-age daughter

Molly Cameron - Director of the Biology Center at LIT

Elaine Ickes - presumed incoming Secretary of DoTI

Emmaline Stutz - ecologist and new DRA member of the committee

Dr. Ralph Manley - the Biology Center's horticulturist

Dr. Marcy Grossman - the raging feminist

Daryl Coker - with his wife, co-owner of the alpaca farm

Chuck Hadaman - prominent resident of the town of Bella Villa, Chief of Facilities at DoTI, and metal fabricator *extraordinaire*

Daryl Coker, Jr. - son of the Cokers

Sandy Coker - Junior's wife

Claudia Coker - with her husband, co-owner of the alpaca farm

Sam - sheriff of Bella Villa county

Dr. Bessie Lee - Pie's wife and an archeologist

Buddy - the grocer

Duane – waiter, maitre d', and proprietor of the Rabbit Hole

PROLOGUE

May 1992

It was an oddly matched pair, walking through the wetland. Both were shod appropriately in waterproof boots, both were covered in mosquito repellant, both were wearing loose, water-resistant clothing. One of them, a botanist, was a very small man – barely five feet. Tiny hands. Boots probably purchased in the kids department. The other surveyor was reasonably tall – about five ten or eleven – but seemed huge next to the botanist. They each carried a "sharpshooter," a heavy, narrow shovel used when taking samples for soils and wetland surveys.

They made their way slowly, taking soil samples and filling out forms, examining the flora, listening for bird calls. "Hey," the little botanist exclaimed, "that sounds like a least bittern. Look over there at about eight o'clock. See that spot of orange? I think that's him." They pointed their binoculars toward the sound.

The little bird, the smallest of the North American herons, was huddled in the grasses of the marsh. The two of them grinned and low-fived – at least the tall one low-fived. It was kind of a middle-five for the little botanist.

They moved slowly through the wetland, the little botanist

skipping ahead, bending down every now and then to examine an interesting plant or to dig up a soil sample, and then darting away to repeat the process a bit further on.

"Holy crap," he shouted. "Look at this!"

The other surveyor caught up. The little botanist was beside himself with excitement. Literally jumping up and down. He was pointing at a clump of flowers. "Look. Look. *Cypripedium candidum*. Small white lady's slipper orchids. A whole field of the suckers! They're damn near extinct. Man, wait'll we tell the Society what we found. What a find!"

The tall surveyor bent down and examined one of the flowers, nearly as excited as the little botanist. "C'mon, let's get this written and published before someone beats us to it."

The two of them turned back, the little botanist moving ahead excitedly, bending every once in a while to examine leaves that could be of the orchid. The tall surveyor following closely behind, raised the sharpshooter and brought it down, hard, on the back of the little botanist's head. The botanist went down. The tall surveyor turned him over, stamped on his throat, removed all of his clothing, picked him up, carried him deep into the marsh, took the little guy's sharpshooter, and departed.

It was weeks before the little botanist was found and by then there wasn't much left of him.

CHAPTER 1

May 18, 1992

I leaned up against the back fender of the Mustang and waited for Alex to finish nuzzling Gertrude, the gray, 9-month old alpaca weanling. He scratched her ears and gave her a final smooch on her nose. "So long, Gertie, we'll see you next week."

The critter made a little humming noise. Alex reached into his pocket and gave her an apple slice. Appeased, she took the fruit and boogied off to link up with the herd.

When Alex joined me at the Mustang, I took hold of his ears and gave him a smooch on his nose. "Hmmm," he said, "Do you think we can be a little late for work today?"

"No, you have a staff meeting." I reached into my pocket and gave him an apple slice.

"I'm married to a screwball!" he cried. But he ate the fruit.

We climbed into the car and headed for the office. My turn to drive.

Alex and I both work for the Laboratory for Industrial Technology (LIT), which is part of the U.S Department of Trade and Industry (DoTI – aptly called "dotty"). Alex heads up the Computer Sciences Center. (Biological Sciences is the other Center.) I'm a Management Scientist in the Director's office.

We've been married for about a year and the novelty hasn't yet worn off. Since we're *both* screwballs, I doubt if it will ever wear off.

The reason we're consorting with alpacas is that we have a little weekend cabin on an alpaca farm. On Mondays, we have a short commute, up a winding country road to the LIT building in rural Maryland. The rest of the week we have a long commute from Old Town Alexandria in urban Virginia. We've thought about moving closer to LIT – we have friends in the nearby town of Bella Villa. We even looked at houses in Bella Villa. But we finally decided that we like living in Old Town. We like going to the movies or to a play on a weekday night. We like poking around the shops. We like the abundance of good restaurants. And besides, if the winter weather is rotten, we can reside in the cabin until the roads get passable.

Alex said, "Bill Clinton is going to win this election. Will the change in administration cause any upheavals in the upper reaches of LIT?"

"I doubt it. Pie knows the probable incoming Secretary of DoTI as well as he knows the outgoing one, so he'll still be in the inner circle. With a new administration, there'll obviously be changes in economic and trade policy, and the new vice president is a bear on the environment and climate change, so there'll be upheavals in those quarters. But nothing that will impact LIT."

Famous last words.

We had just about reached the LIT building when a line of stopped cars halted our progress. Joe, one of Sheriff Sam's deputies, approached.

"What's going on, Joe? Serious accident?" Alex asked.

"Naw, this won't take long. We're just trying to bring some emergency vehicles through. Fat lot of good they'll do, though. The victim's deader than a door nail."

"What happened?" I asked.

Joe shook his head. "A woman was killed on that little road above Bella Villa. Biology teacher at the high school. A motorist saw her car stopped in the middle of the road. Motorist got out of his car to see what the matter was and there she was with her throat cut, lying next to the car. Thing is, most of us knew her. She'd been at the school since Hector was a pup and we've all taken biology from her.

"I suppose it shouldn't be, but it's worse when it's someone you knew."

"Geez," Alex commiserated. "Any clue as to why it happened?"

"Dunno," Joe said. "Her clothes were mussed, but until we get some tests done, we won't know if it was rape. She stopped her car and got out for some reason. Some low-life probably pretended to need help and when she got out of the car, attacked her. But why?" He shrugged.

"The county's never had anything like this happen before – at least not in the nine years that I've been a deputy. And like I said, you feel worse about it when it was someone you knew."

Sirens were heard.

"Sounds like the emergency guys are coming through. I'll move my cruiser and let the traffic flow."

I pulled into the LIT parking lot. We checked our watches and decided that we had time for a quick snoggle before we had to go to our offices. We had barely begun the snoggle when there came a rapping on the window. We glared in that direction. Don, my companion in the Director's office, grinned back. Alex lowered the window and stuck his head out.

Don said, "After you finish renewing your acquaintance, send Bea to Pie's office." He   walked off before we could ask him what was up.

Abandoning our truncated snoggle, Alex and I got out of the car and went our separate ways. I stopped in my office just long enough to shed my jacket. I met Don on the way to Pie's place.   "Whassup?"

"Interesting event. Pie called me last night.   He tried to get you but you don't have a phone in your rustic retreat."

We greeted Lenore, who waved us in to Pie's office.   In an excess of zeal, Lenore had requisitioned a large sofa with throw pillows for his room.   While the newly acquired furnishings were quite nice – upholstered in a gentle, teal blue – we were at a loss as to where they came from.   They were in good condition, but obviously not new.   Our best guess is that some self-important bureaucrat in an administration gone-bye had splurged on his office and a more spartan successor had replaced the furniture. Lenore must have rummaged in the Department's used-furniture warehouse before finding something she considered suitable for someone of Pie's eminence.   And it did, in fact, suit the ambiance.

Pie was perched on the edge of his desk, awaiting us. The eminent Dr. P.I. Lee, aka Pie, was recruited for his position by the current Secretary of DoTI.   My first (deceased) husband, Harry, and I were the honorary niece and nephew of Uncle Pie and Aunt Bessie.   I could hardly believe it when he was appointed to take the place of the former LIT director. My dream of a boss come true.

Pie is a microbiologist of considerable renown. DoTI snatched him from the jaws of MIT, where he held forth as a Distinguished Professor. He's a member of the National Academy of Sciences; chairman of the President's Commission on Scientific Exchange with the People's Republic of China; recipient of the Biotechnology Society Pioneer Award; and on and on.   The Secretary of DoTI lured him to LIT on the grounds that his country needed him.   In truth, he took the job because he thought it would be fun.

The offspring of a Chinese mathematician father and a Jewish housewife mother, Pie is the most elegant man I have ever met. His silver hair is brushed, his shoes shined, knife-edged creases for his trousers. The illusion is shattered by his perfectly ridiculous Brooklyn accent.

All this in contrast to Don.   Don Cromarty is a big,   loose-jointed, shambling guy who would probably leave the house in his pajamas if Connie, his wife, didn't make sure that he was dressed in daytime clothes with the buttons aligned properly. Don just doesn't think of those things. His passion is softball.   He plays softball – right field where they put good hitters who can't run or field – and he coaches little league.   Don used to be my boss, but he schemed, lobbied, pleaded, and finally got me promoted to the Senior Executive Service.   Lots of women have told me of the glass ceiling they hit when promotions are handed out.   Their misfortune is that they don't have a rabbi like Don.   Don sat in one of the visitors' chairs.   I sank into the sofa.

The three of us manage the "corporate" aspect of LIT as opposed to the "operational" aspect, which is the province of the Center Directors. Together, we formulate policy.   Are we going in the right direction?   Are the Centers focused on areas that have major impacts on trade and industry or are some of their people playing in sandboxes?   All three of us are devotees of Management by Walking Around. I spend a lot of time visiting the Centers and shmoozing – identifying problems and providing pats on the back.   Don does the numbers.   It's up to him to provide a draft budget that encompasses all of our monetary needs and indicates where, God forbid, cuts will have to be made.   I'm responsible for the day-to-day relations with Congress and with the Office of Management and Budget. This requires a great deal more schmoozing. By the time Congress considers the Nation's budget, I will have gathered much information about the concerns of those people, and when Pie is called to testify, he knows enough to push the right buttons. The three of us split the endless "High Level Committees" – many of which are a waste of time.

"It's like this," Pie began, "Despite what Gallup says, all of the insider polls say that Clinton will win. I was told that the expected incoming Administration has decided to take global warming seriously and they want to set up a joint committee of DoTI and the Department of Rural Affairs to determine the probable effects of the climate change on agricultural-type matters and the resultant effect on our trade balance. Bea, *bubele*, you're looking confused."

"Not about the seriousness of global warming, but what does that have to do with LIT?"

"The incoming Secretary wants you to lead the DoTI team."

"Come on! I don't know anything about trade or industry. My job is to herd scientists and cater to your every whim. The person doesn't even know me."

Don laughed. "Maybe that's why she chose you."

She? So Don knew who the new Secretary would be.

I threw one of the tasteful teal pillows at him. Still laughing, he fielded it. If he keeps that up, his team may move him to left.

"Now children." admonished Pie. "She wants you because she's got a good idea who'll represent DRA. They'll be headed by a sexist idiot and she thinks it'll be good for him to be outranked by a woman."

"Great. Doesn't DoTI have a senior woman who knows something about at least one of the subjects?"

"Yeah," Pie said, "but they're all assigned to other committees." He wrinkled his forehead. "It's the same in the universities. There are too few senior women to serve on all of the committees. So the women who *are* there are assigned to many, many committees. That's so that the administration can claim that women are represented in all aspects of University governance. The senior women are always pooped."

"Well," I asked, knowing full well that the battle was lost, "doesn't DRA have a senior woman?"

"That's what I asked Elaine. She said, 'DRA? You gotta be kidding.'"

"Okay. I give. What's the next step?"

"Do you know anyone at DoTI whom you'd like on the team?"

"Let me think about it. I'm on so many committees I'm sure I must know some good candidates." Said with a straight face.

"So cater to one of my many whims and stop being a wisenheimer."

Don and I laughed. "How big a team?" I asked.

"Three, including you.

"Let me know as soon as you have them identified. The Secretaries have set up the first meeting at two o'clock tomorrow at Cabot House."

"Tomorrow?"

"You got it. The 'request' came from the Clinton team. They're cooperating with the current Secretaries. The current guys aren't admitting that Clinton will win, but they think the Committee's a good idea and say they'll implement it after the election."

"I'd better start searching my Roll-o-Dex."

I got up to leave. Don stayed to discuss budget with Pie.

Leonore hailed me as I left Pie's office. "Jim Daley called. His wife died this weekend. He won't be in today."

"Oh no. Poor Jim."

"Well, maybe." Lenore looked owlishly at me.

"What does that mean?"

"Nothing. Forget I said it."

Unlike most devotees of the rumor mill, Lenore's information is usually correct. Something was definitely up. But if Lenore decided to keep her mouth shut, shut it would stay.

"Okay. Thanks, Lenore."

I walked back to my office wondering who could handle Jim's duties until he recovered sufficiently to return. He was the guy on my staff who handled Congressional inquiries and who showed visitors – particularly school groups – around the joint. A big blond guy, he has a unique sense of humor. He's been known to greet the school groups while wearing an Albert Einstein rubber mask and speaking in what he claims is an Austrian accent. The rest of us think he sounds like the Swedish chef. The kids adore him.

There are two and a half additional members of my staff. Jeanne Cameron handles travel, oversees the support staff, and takes care of non-sensitive personnel matters. Jeanne is a comfortable, fortyish woman who is invariably calm, always tactful, and can be counted on to defuse any incendiary happening.

Marge Dunn takes care of publications. A carrot-topped beauty, she is as perfect an editor as can be found anywhere. Not only does she know her stuff as an editor, she knows how to deal with scientists. Both other agencies (offering promotions) and private sector companies (offering untold riches), are intent on stealing her from us. But she remains at LIT.   She doesn't need the money; she's married to a retired Microsoft millionaire and she loves her job here.

I split Ben Goldfarb with Don.   He does budget with Don and analysis of trade statistics with me.   Normally a sweet-tempered man, he becomes a monster of a micromanager when it comes to dealing with the support staff.   Therefore, he is allowed to deal with typists only through Jeanne.   He has taken that rule philosophically.   He is also an inveterate punster.   Which is why we don't allow him to deal with the outside world – particularly members of Congress.

One or more of us would have to handle Jim's duties until he returned. Well, I'd get to that after I identified my Committee-mates.

I put my feet up on my desk, and pondered.   There would be only six of us on the committee.   DRA would select the obvious.   Certainly an agronomist.   Probably a botanist. Maybe an ecologist. Maybe a soil scientist.   I don't want warring specialists, so what's left for us? One good thing – if the Republican Secretaries of DRA and DoTI are cooperating with the presumed Democratic Secretaries of DRA and DoTI, I don't have to consider the political orientation of the Committee members.

Fisheries would be a good addition.   In the grand scheme of things, fish don't count for much in U.S. trade, but what there is of it is extremely important to certain areas (read Congressional districts) of the country. Whatever else global warming affects, most (if not all) of the marine biologists believe the oceans will rise, which will certainly affect the fishing industry – for good or ill.

How about someone who knows about trees, a forester or a silviculturist?   My guess is that DRA will do what DoTI did – that is, pick a team leader and let *him* (at DRA unlikely to be *her*) pick the other two members. If so, he'll probably forget that the United States has forests.

I grabbed the Roll-o-Dex and riffled through it. Billy Norman was an expert on the fisheries industry. Good guy. Cooperative committee member.

I continued riffling. No one jumped out of the forest. I walked down to Ben's office. He was sitting there, resplendent in a shiny, taupe, polyester suit. Under the suit was a bright yellow shirt. The shirt was enhanced by an Elmer Fudd tie – one of my favorites among Ben's assortment of neckwear.

I explained the problem. "What would you think of Fisheries and Silviculture as committee members?"

"Will DRA provide the boring members?"

"Most likely."

"Then Fisheries and Silviculture would be good. Who do you have in mind?"

"Billy Norman for Fisheries. I don't have a Forestry contact at DoTI."

"Get Julia Han. Lovely soft-spoken lady and a steel magnolia if ever there was one. She can hold her own without causing problems."

"You are a pearl without price, Goldfarb.

"Did you know that Jim's wife died?"

Ben winced. "That poor guy. Well, at least his kid's in college. He won't have to cope with an adolescent."

"I'm going to get together with Marge and Jeanne to figure out how to cover his duties."

"Anything I can do?"

"I don't think you can spare the time. But stand by for statistical consultation if a Congressional inquiry comes through."

"Hokay. Fear not. I've got the Congress's number."

Please, God, I prayed as I left Ben's office, *don't let him near a Member.*

I returned to my desk and after checking to see what Jim had on his calendar (thankfully no escort duties scheduled for today) I called Marge and Jeanne and asked them to meet me in the small conference room after lunch. Then I looked up Norman and Han, made notes for Pie, and went to meet him and Don in the LIT cafeteria.

I picked up a plate of meatloaf and a rhubarb crumble and joined them. Pie swallowed a bite of his meatloaf. "Did you identify some Committee members?"

"I think so." I handed him the notes. "Do you think I should check with our Bio Center before we propose my selections? My and Ben's selections, I should say. I know Norman and Ben knows Han and thinks highly of her."

Pie shook his head. "Let's go with what you got. Bio might propose a botanist and that could lead to friction if DRA also produces one."

"Agreed," I said. "Could you ask Lenore to let Han and Norman know that they've been selected for the honor?"

Pie nodded.

"Do you guys know about Jim's wife?"

"Yeah," said Don. "Lenore told us. She's being cagy. Maybe she thinks he bumped her off."

At just that point Ben joined us. "Who bumped whom off?"

Don looked at him fondly. "If you repeat one word of that beyond this table, I will bump off *youm.*"

Pie patted Ben on the head. "No, he won't. He's a manager.

He'll delegate it."

We talked desultorily while Ben finished his lunch.

Back in my office, I determined that Marge and Jeanne had eaten lunch and joined them in the small conference room. Jim had two school groups scheduled for the next day.

"I can take the one in the morning," I said. "But in the afternoon I have a Committee meeting."

Jeanne volunteered to take the afternoon group. Marge would take the phone calls. "I wonder how long he'll be out," Marge mused.

"No telling," I remarked. "He's got a girl in college. If this hits her hard, it might be more than a week. I think Jim will want to be there for her if she needs him."

"Can Ben cover some of Jim's stuff?" Jeanne asked.

Marge and I looked at her. Then we thought of a conversation Ben might have with a Congressional staffer or, heaven forbid, with a Member. Then we thought about Ben and a school group. The three of us started to laugh.

"Oh," said Jeanne, "of course he can't."

"Ben is primed to be a consultant for you if you need statistical help. I can take the school groups as long as Pie has nothing urgent for me. If he does need me for something else, Jeanne can take them. Unless you two would rather take turns at the tasks."

Marge and Jeanne looked at one another and shook their heads. "It won't be for too long a time, so let's leave it as it is."

"Good. If anything you can't handle comes up and I'm not available, call Don."

I returned to my office to discover three neatly typed four-by-five cards waiting for me. Lenore had unearthed the names of the DRA committee members and had plumbed her inexhaustible pool of informants for the skinny on each of them.

The senior member of the DRA team is G. Douglas Mapledent, PhD. His rank is GS-15 [the highest civil service rank before the Senior Executive Service]. Dr. Mapledent is a botanist. He was born in Alabama and retains his southern accent. There are mixed reviews from the DRA secretaries and typists. They all say he is very charming and courteous. Several of them obviously adore him. Others say he is a patronizing creep who has a serious problem with roving hands. He is a demanding supervisor who micromanages both the professionals and the support staff. He does not appreciate women in high places.

Ronald Drumm, PhD, is a soil scientist. His rank is GS-14. He comes from the coal mining region of Pennsylvania. The secretaries and typists say his fingernails are always dirty and he smells ripe. They do do not like him and do not trust him. They say that things like rulers and staplers tend to disappear after he has been near the typing pool. He is often rude. He is the opposite of Dr. Mapledent, who is meticulous about proofing the secretaries' work. Dr. Drumm accepts whatever he is given. On occasion, a typist will deliberately misspell a word to give a sentence a risque meaning. Either Dr. Drumm does not notice or he does not care.

Howard Farrington III is an agronomist. His rank is GS-14. H e is new to DRA so the secretaries and typists do not know much about him. He came to DRA from an agricultural-type agency in Illinois. He seems like a nice guy. He really cares about his work. Sometimes he stops at a typist's desk and tells her about what he is working on. He is such a nice guy that all of the secretaries and typists pretend that they know what he is talking about.

I wondered if there was a Lenore-type at DRA and if so, did she get the skinny on the LIT team? And if she did, did she share it with Mapledent? I'd find out soon enough.

I called Lenore and thanked her for the cards.

"By the way," she said, "when I was researching Dr. Mapledent, his unit's typist asked about you."

"And may I ask what you told her?"

"Nothing important. Just that you were competent, polite, and very serious."

I laughed. "And you didn't mention that I'm a screwball?"

"Dr. Mapledent can find that out for himself."

She hung up.

At five thirty, Alex met me at the car and we headed for Alexandria.

The junction of our country road and the highway featured a number of mismatched enterprises, including a used tire emporium, a raunchy looking bar, a cut-rate gas station, and a disgusting Alligator Wrestling and Snake Exhibit – live see 'em live. I always look in the other direction. I Hate Snakes.

Once past and safely on the highway, Alex asked, "Do you want to go to the talkies tonight?"

"What's on?"

"Two good ones. *The Silence of the Lambs* and *Thelma and Louise*."

We spent the next half hour discussing the pros and cons of the two movies. We finally tossed a coin. *The Silence of the Lambs.*

We got home a little after seven, which gave us time for a meal at the Taverna Cretekou before the nine o'clock show. Normally, when watching a movie, Alex and I catch up on any snoggles we may have missed during the day. Not with this movie. We were both scared spitless.

CHAPTER 2

May 19, 1992

Alex and I mopped up our pancakes, put the dishes in the dishwasher, and headed out to the Mustang. Alex's turn to drive.

It was a gorgeous day. Almost seventy degrees and the sun shining. "Top down?"

"Top down," I agreed.

We started off with Alex, in full voice, running through his extensive repertory of Gilbert and Sullivan. He had reached *When the Foeman Bares his Steel* when he stopped at a red light, next to a Porsche convertible.

Alex: When the foeman bares his steel

Me: Tarantara! Tarantara!

Alex: We uncomfortable feel

Me: Tarantara! T arantara!

Alex: And we find the wisest thing

Me and the guy in the Porsche: Tarantara! Taranta...

At which point we were interrupted by a cacophony of horn blasts from all the cars behind us.

End of concert as the two convertibles jack-rabbited off. W e waved good-bye to the Porsche as it turned onto the beltway and we continued toward our country road.

"That's too bad," Alex said. "it sounded better with the bigger chorus."

We continued our Gilbert and Sullivan program as we wound up

18

the road. Once past the Alligator Wrestling place, it's a lovely drive, especially in the spring. Wild columbines and geraniums, black-eyed susans and oxeye daisies line the road. Apple blossoms add to the display. We were enjoying ourselves mightily until we were stopped behind a long line of cars. Deputy Joe appeared.

"Hey Joe," Alex said, "Now what?"

"Motorcycle met up with a UPS truck. Kid on the cycle was killed and the UPS driver is in shock."

"How did it happen?" I asked.

"The dumb kid was trying to do a superman at sixty miles an hour around a curve."

"A superman?"

Joe looked disgusted. "That's when the motorcycle driver grabs hold of the handlebars and kicks his legs up and back so that he looks like superman flying."

Alex asked, "Someone would do that for real?"

Joe nodded. "For real. The idiot kid bought it and the poor UPS guy is going to have to live the rest of his life knowing he killed someone."

"Shit!" Alex said.

"Couldn't have put it better myself. This may take another half hour to clear up. I better get back to the action."

Joe walked back to the mess.

"Oh, oh," I said, "I'm supposed to take Jim's school group at nine thirty. No way I'm going to make it and no way I can let anyone know. With hope, when the kiddies show up someone will call Pie's office and Lenore will alert Marge or Jeanne."

"Every cloud has a silver lining," remarked Alex, nuzzling my ear.

We unhooked our seat belts and settled in for a serious snoggle.

Alex pulled into the LIT parking lot. I was out of the car and running before he turned off the motor. My phone rang as soon as I reached my office. It was Jeanne.

"Bea, Jim came in today and took his morning tour. When you hadn't arrived by nine thirty, I went to the lobby and Albert Einstein was there with one of Alex's crew who was wearing a Cookie Monster mask."

This was a bit much to absorb. "Jim is in? The Cookie Monster?"

"Yes and yes. The school kids are fourth graders. They looked like they were loving it."

"Sheesh. There was an accident in front of us and we sat in the car for over half an hour before we could move. Thanks for covering. If Jim hadn't appeared things would have gone south if you hadn't been there. Fourth graders are not known for their patience.

"After Jim finishes the tour I'll find out why he came into the office just a few days after his wife died."

I hung up, consulted the DoTI directory and rang Julia Han, my silviculturist. As it happened, Billy Norman, the Fisheries guy, was in her office. They were speculating about the Committee and their roles as members. We decided that I would pick them up at one o'clock in front of Han's building. The three of us could continue the discussion as we drove to Cabot House.

I thought for a minute. If I take the car, Alex will be wheel-less if he needs to go someplace before I get back. I called Lenore and arranged to have a government car delivered to the LIT parking lot.

Like several other Federal departments (The Department of

Energy, for instance), DoTI is decentralized – at least physically. The main administrative offices are located in D.C. while mission offices are spread all over the place. Most trade-and-industry related agricultural activities are in a building a couple of miles south of LIT. This group had close ties to DRA, which has a building just north of LIT. Billy Norman and Fisheries, on the other hand, work closely with the National Oceanic and Atmospheric Administration (NOAA). Billy's group is housed on the Eastern Shore of the Chesapeake Bay. It was just dumb luck that Billy was in Han's office when I called.

I wandered down to Ben's office and asked him to get me some Fisheries and Forests import/export data. It will be important to remind people just how much global warming will affect our industries and our trade position.

Jim was in my office, waiting for me, when I returned.

"Jim, what on earth are you doing in the office so soon?"

"I love my job, Bea," he said simply.

He looked uncomfortable. Then, "Bea, can I talk to you about personal stuff? It's okay if you don't want me to. I'd understand."

"Don't be silly. Of course you can talk to me."

He didn't say anything for a bit. Then, "I didn't love my wife, Bea. I didn't even like her. I used to love her, but she got weird. Religious weird. We're Catholics. So first she started helping with our church's flower arrangements. Then she started going to Mass and confession two or three times every day. I think our priest kind of questioned her about that – I'm not sure – but she started rotating around the various Catholic churches. Then she moved into the spare bedroom saying that she was married to Jesus. It's been like that for a couple of years. I'm finding it hard to grieve. I'll go through the motions, of course. Chrissie, my daughter, is helping with the funeral arrangements and all that stuff. She's a competent kid. She's a sophomore at the University of Maryland."

"Couldn't you get an annulment on the grounds of psychic incapacity?"

"I suppose I could have. But I just couldn't do that to Chrissie. I mean, her mother's a nut but Chrissie doesn't know that and she shouldn't have to know that."

"What can I do to help, Jim?"

"Two things, if you would. First, just let me come back to work with no fuss. I belong here."

"Yes, you do."

"Then, could Chrissie come talk to you? She needs a woman role model. God forbid," he smiled, "she should take after her mother."

I laughed. "But you want her to take after a screwball? Okay, if you're willing to risk it. I've just been put on a committee and I don't have the schedule yet. Our first meeting is today at Cabot House. Can you find out right away when Chrissie can be here? If necessary, I'll tell the Committee that I have a previous appointment for that time."

Jim got up. "Thanks. She's at home now. I'll call her as soon as I get back to my office."

I walked to Pie's office, stopping at Lenore's desk to thank her for arranging the car. "How do you do that? Whenever I try to order a car myself I get all sorts of reasons why I can't have one for several days."

Lenore donned her virtuous look. "You don't have enough friends in low places."

In all the years I've known her, this was the first time I'd ever heard her make a joke. Shaken by Lenore's departure from character, I entered Pie's office.

He and Don were engaged in the never-ending budget discussion.

"*Nu*," asked Pie, "*vos makhstu?*"

"Jim came in today.   Said he'd rather be here than home.   He asked if I'd talk with his daughter.   She's a sophomore at Maryland.   If she seems suitable, can we find room in the budget to offer her a summer internship?"

"Yeah," Don answered.   "Interns don't cost much."

"Good idea," Pie said.

"I'll let you know how my talk with her comes out.   I'm going to grab a sandwich and then pick up my Committee-mates.   We'll drive to Cabot House together.   See you guys tomorrow."

I stopped at my office and found a note from Jim.   Chrissie could come over any time tomorrow.   I called Jim and asked him to deliver Chrissie when he came in.

Then I trotted to the cafeteria, picked up a grilled cheese sandwich, and went off to find my government car. I managed not to dribble cheese on the upholstery.

Now, the mention of a government car conjures up the image of a sleek, black limo bearing the President or a foreign dignitary to some glamorous destination.   Erase the image; it's not like that.

Like the sleek, black limos, the normal government car is delivered very clean.   There the similarity ends.   The government car is usually cream colored.   It is several years old.   It has a heater that does not work. Some of them have air conditioners.   They don't work either.   There is no radio.   To make up for the lack of a radio, the cars produce a number of intriguing, if not identifiable, noises.   Not too long ago, the wheel of the car I was driving came off while I was motoring up a winding country road.   The car that now awaited me was a typical government car.

I got in, turned the key, and a few blasphemous words later, the miserable bolt-bucket started.   With the car emitting various gasps and groans, I drove back down the country road, noting the roiled spot where the motorcycle accident had occurred, and turned right onto the well-maintained road that led to the DoTI building.   There were a number of people milling around in front of the place, enjoying the noonday sun. I spotted Billy and a woman I took to be Julia Han standing a little apart from the crowd.

After some discussion as to who would sit in the back seat (Han would –   Norman needed what leg room the front seat afforded) they clambered in. Julia Han was a small, very beautiful, Oriental woman. Despite her diminutive size, she did not look at all fragile.   I don't know why, but she gave the impression that she could deck a horse.

Billy was larger but not large – about Alex's five foot eight in length.   He was considerably rounder than Alex.   Not obese but, well– round.   He had dark, curly hair and usually wore an affable expression. "It's good to see you again, Bea.   Last time I saw you, you weren't married and you weren't in the Senior Executive Service. Congratulations on both counts."

"Thanks.   How're your wife and kids – if I remember rightly you had two of them.   Kids not wives."

"All's well.   My boy is a senior in high school and got accepted to UVA.   My girl is in her last year at middle school.   And you wouldn't believe my wife."

"What's she doing?"

"Painting.   She's a photorealist and damn good at it.   The Hirschhorn is taking one of her paintings."   Billy was so proud I thought

24

he would bust a button.

"What about you, Julia? Are you married?"

"Engaged." She made a face. "Coping with a traditional Chinese family. Warren is Caucasian and they don't like it a bit. But – we shall overcome." She grinned.

I had no doubt that Julia Han would overcome anything in her path.

Someone in the Secretary's office had briefed both Billy and Julia on the purpose of the Committee and they were excited about joining it. Julia said, "It's about time we started planning for the meltdown. We've still got time, but not a lot of it. Will we do the study in-house or will we need contractors?"

"That's one of the things the Committee will have to recommend. I'd vote for contractors – probably several universities. If we do it in-house we'll be more vulnerable to changes in the administration and Congress. The universities have their members of Congress looking after them. A change in administration won't alter that."

"I think you're right," Billy agreed. "There may be problems integrating their work, but it's do-able."

"Do I take it," I asked "that we agree that global warming is a fact and that we should try to ameliorate the effects?'

"Of course." Julia looked puzzled. "What's not to agree?"

"There's controversy at DRA," I answered. "Roughly, the positions are first, 'global warming is a myth; this is just a cyclical phenomenon that happens every three or four hundred years'; second, 'global warming is real, but humans have done nothing to cause it and there is nothing humans can do about it'; third, 'global warming is real and humans have either caused it or caused it to accelerate and humans can do something about it.'

"Then, among those who believe that humans had something to do with causing global warming and can do something to fix it, there's a heated argument going on as to whether global warming is good or bad for agriculture.

"I have no idea where the members of the DRA team stand. For all I know, the controversy may permeate their team."

By this time, we were traveling the road toward LIT. Every mile or so, the car gave a little jump, which added a bit of excitement to the journey. I took the Bella Villa turn-off, drove through the little town and eventually came to a discreet sign, *Cabot House,* with an arrow pointing right.

I turned onto a narrow lane that wound gently through the countryside for about three miles. Cabot House was at the end of the road. Signs directed us to a small parking lot. Two cars were in the lot – a newish Nissan and a Jeep. I pulled in alongside the Jeep and we debarked.

Cabot House was impressive, in an Old New England, Old Money way. A rambling, wooden building, it was painted creamy white with gray accents. A front lawn, disciplined by stone hedging, was reached by two steps. A sign pointed toward a handicapped ramp at the side of the building. The lawn itself was host to a stylish Japanese red maple, several azalea bushes displaying large, pale rose blooms, a bank of lenten-roses of similar hue, and a splurge of glorious, pale rose parrot tulips. It was odds on that the display would change with the seasons.

A flagstone path wound through the lawn area to several more steps ending in an extensive front porch furnished with wicker rockers, armchairs, and end tables.

The front door opened and a tall, slim Black man in a beautifully tailored dark blue suit greeted us. He held out his hand. "I'm Dexter Hamilton. I'm the manager of Cabot House. Welcome."

We took turns shaking his hand.

"Your colleagues are already in the small conference room enjoying some coffee and pastries. They asked me to show you to the room when you arrived. But you each have a sitting room of your own, so you can shake off the effects of the drive before you meet them."

Han, Norman, and I consulted our respective watches. It was ten to two on all of them.

"I think we'll say 'hello' first and then excuse ourselves for a quick wash. There shouldn't be an objection. We're a little early."

Hamilton nodded. We followed him through an elegantly appointed foyer. *Was that a genuine Tiffany chandelier?* He pointed toward a corridor to the left off the foyer. "The individual rooms are down there. Your names are on the doors."

He led us to the right of the foyer and into a wood-paneled room that contained a round walnut conference table, surrounded by six chairs, and a walnut breakfront containing an assortment of Waterford crystal. Mapledent, Drumm, and Farrington occupied three of the chairs.

"Would you like coffee, tea, or some other beverage?" Hamilton asked us late arrivals. Billy and I opted for coffee. Julia asked for tea.

"Would you like Keemun or would you prefer something lighter in the afternoon?"

"I'll take the Keemun, thank you." She smiled at Hamilton. "I need something to wake me up after that drive."

Hamilton smiled back. "We started brewing so that it would be ready when you arrived." His smile broadened. "It's good to have you back with us. I'm looking forward to your wedding.

27

"Do you and Warren have plans for Memorial Day? The little town of Bella Villa usually has a fine parade and pig roast if that interests you."

"Thank you, Dexter. We have plans for this year but we'll make it to Bella Villa for sure next year."

Hamilton nodded and withdrew.

Julia had not mentioned her acquaintance with the mansion. Good for her.

Mapledent stood up to greet us. He was a handsome man. Standing somewhere between five ten and six feet, he was a well-proportioned guy. Broad shoulders, slim waist, graying hair with white wings, cut just a tad longer than regulation. His eyes were so blue that the color was evident even from across the table. "Sit down, sit down."

"We'd like to wash up before we get down to business," I said.

"Certainly," 'Suhtenly' in Mapledent-speak. "But sit for just a minute while we introduce ourselves and I sketch the program."

We sat.

" I am Dr. G. Douglas Mapledent. Now, because DRA is the lead agency, I will chair this group." He looked at me. "I'm sure you will have no objection to that, little lady."

Billy's head jerked up and he opened his mouth.

I shook my head at him and remained pleasantly mute. Billy subsided.

"This tough looking hombre to my left," Mapledent continued, "is Dr. Ronald Drumm. He's a soil scientist and to my right is Mr. Howard Farrington, our agronomist. Now your turn, little lady."

"I'm Dr. Beatrice Goode. Dr. Julia Han is a silviculturist. Dr.

Billy Norman handles Fisheries."

Mapledent's eyebrows rose at the mention of Fisheries, but he did not comment on that, only said, "That settled, the agenda for the day will be a quick tour of the grounds – I will lead the tour – then a short discussion of what our Mission statement should be.   Once we have that discussion, which should take some time, we will adjourn and reassemble next week in the morning of Tuesday, the twenty sixth, and hammer out the Mission statement, move on to the Objectives, and establish a governance structure for the committee."

I stood up.   "Now, if you don't mind, we'll wash up."

"Certainly.   Let us meet on the front porch at two thirty for the tour."

Julia smiled her sweet smile.   "I don't need a tour, Dr. Mapledent..."

"Please call me Doug, sweetie."

"All right, Doug." I noticed that she didn't invite him to call her Julia.

"I don't need a tour.   Since you were here early, you have probably shown your group the sights already.   So I'll take the DoTI folk around the place and we'll meet you back here at about three thirty."

We left the room before he could object.

"Let's meet in my room," I said.

We found my room and entered.   It was a comfortable sitting room.   It contained a leather couch, two matching armchairs, and a glass-topped coffee table.   A working fireplace was tucked into a corner. Wood was piled on the hearth. A very good reproduction of Bellows' *Mountain Farm* hung on the wall behind the couch.

As soon as the door was closed, Billy exploded.   "Are you going to let that son of a bitch get away with taking over the committee?"

"Of course not. Sit down."

Julia and Billy took the armchairs, leaving me the couch.

I explained, "He's a son of a bitch, but he's not a stupid son of a bitch. If I object now, he'll turn the objection into an argument between DoTI and DRA. We've all been in the government long enough to know that neither of the Secretaries will back down. I'm pretty sure that he made up that nonsense about DRA being the lead agency; this Committee was set up to be a cooperative venture. In fact, I was specifically assigned to this committee because my management thought it would be good for Mapledent to have to report to a woman. I'll get this settled tomorrow."

There was a knock on the door. I opened it and found a matronly woman with a cart bearing our coffee and tea service. "Mr. Hamilton thought you might be here. Is it all right if I come in?'

"Of course." She entered, delivered goodies, and departed.

When she had closed the door behind her, Julia asked. "What do you think will happen?" She took a swallow of tea.

"At least four possible outcomes that I can think of and probably a few that haven't occurred to me. Most likely is that I'll head up the committee with Mapledent reporting to me. Second is that I'll head up the committee and Mapledent will have been replaced. Third is that DoTI will secede from the union and we'll do an independent investigation of the effects of climate change on trade and industry. Fourth and least likely, our Secretary will cave and my Director will take me off the Committee."

Julia grinned. "Chief, I salute you."

"Thank you." I nibbled on a pastry. "What does that tea taste like?"

"Here, take a sip." She handed me her cup. I sipped.

"Wow. Where do you get it?"

"At Teaism in the District. And give me back my cup."

Reluctantly, I returned it.

Billy was happily adding to his girth. "Will we have to write a stupid Mission statement?"

"We won't even write a sensible Mission statement. We don't have time for that nonsense.

"Let's take the tour."

"Wait a minute," Julia said, "while I get my camera."

She returned with an impressive Nikon.

CHAPTER 3

May 19, 1992 (cont.)

We walked out the back door of Cabot House and into a remarkable landscape. A long flight of steps led to a formal garden. Straight ahead was a stone arch through which there was a glimpse of rolling lawn. Before reaching the arch, however, there were wonders to behold. To the right was a rose maze. It was too soon for the rose blooms, but a few early blossoms gave a hint of glory to come.

To the left, tulips were massed in a riot of color. I never knew tulips came in that many colors, sizes, and shapes.

We walked through the arch to find a charming statue of a small girl bent over a pump. The pump was spewing water into a basin in which multi-colored koi were happily swimming. Blooming fruit trees bordered the rolling lawn. In front of the trees, day lilies and iris were bursting their buds. Fountains were sprinkled among the trees. We walked across the lawn, through a little grove of trees and emerged onto a short boardwalk. Julia was assiduously snapping pictures.

On either side of the boardwalk was a trail, forming a loop about 2,000 feet in circumference, beginning from one side of the boardwalk and returning to the other. It bordered a small lake and a marsh. There were lots of cattails, an abundance of lizard's tail, some tall blue flag, sedges, and a few water primroses. Julia pointed out a beaver lodge and another similar lodge that seemed to be made of cattails. Julia said that the cattail lodge had been made by muskrats. There was a plentitude of birds.

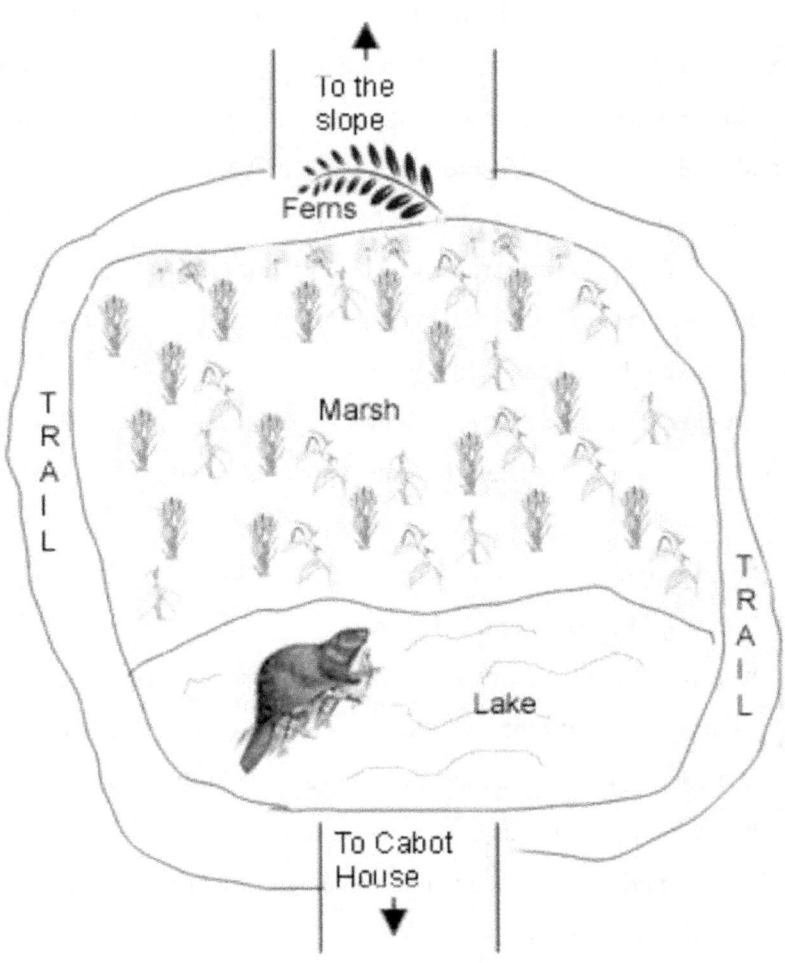

Canada geese (and their disgusting droppings) were all over. Some mallards were swimming around. Overhead were cardinals and redwing blackbirds, among other flying objects. Julia told us that the area housed three types of bat – none of them vampires. There were also turtles. Lots of them. Julia warned us not to wander into their habitat. While usually docile, the snappers become somewhat annoyed if you step on them and are liable to snap. There was a noise that sounded like a demented woodpecker. Julia identified it as coming from a gray tree frog.

We descended the boardwalk to our left and followed the trail.

"The soil around here is called 'marl'. It's clay soil, rich in lime, and it hosts a number of plants that won't readily grow anywhere else. Trillium and jack in the pulpit grow on the edges of the marsh. Wild orchids, lady's slippers, twisted spikerush, pickerel weed – they all love it here.

"The geography here reminds me of New York..."

"New York?" Billy and I chorused.

"Yeah. When you turn a corner it's like you entered a different world. You'll see what I mean when we go around the next curve."

We curved around the marsh and began to approach some relatively dry land, which was covered with ferns.

Julia explained. "Just a very short elevation, maybe two or three inches, and the habitat changes. Neat, isn't it?"

We heard some shouting close by. Not happy shouting.

"You dumb fuck, any one with a brain would know that plants grow better when it gets warmer!"

"Oh yeah, then try planting daisies in a volcanouch!"

We rounded a curve to view Drumm, standing in the ferns, fists clenched, looming over Farrington. Farrington was cradling his nose.

Julia snapped the picture. Ain't telephoto lenses grand?

I touched my companions, put my finger to my lips, and led them back the way we came.

When we were out of earshot I said, "I think we just won the argument. Let's see how Mapledent handles this."

We got back to Cabot House by three o'clock and snuck into my room.

Billy chuckled. "I presume you will let our Secretary know what happened."

"Oh, yes indeed."

Julia looked quite happy. "What do you think will happen?"

"No telling. Drumm will certainly be removed from the Committee. He'll be lucky if Farrington doesn't sue him. Something unfortunate will happen to Mapledent for having the bad judgment to put both of those guys on the DRA team. He must have known they were on opposite sides of a bitter policy argument. He sure won't be running the Committee and might be removed altogether. I just wonder how he'll try to cover this up. He doesn't know we saw the whole thing."

"Let alone took a picture of it." Billy was positively gleeful.

At three thirty we strolled into the conference room. The DRA guys were standing up. Farrington had a patch on his nose.

"I'm sorry, ladies and gentleman, but I am going to have to cut this session short. The Agriculture Ministers of some countries that are very important to us have arrived on short notice, and the team has been summoned back to headquarters.

"Because of this foreshortened meeting, I have arranged for us to meet here this coming Thursday, the twenty first, at two o'clock. I expect you to be here then."

I resisted the temptation to ask him what countries the Ministers were from. The cover story was the best the poor dork could do on the spur of the moment.

We watched them as they got into their cars. Drumm and Mapledent in the Jeep. Farrington in the Nissan. "I'll bet that wasn't the seating arrangement they had when they drove up," Julia said.

Billy added, "That was fun."

By the time I dropped Billy and Julia at the DoTI building and got back to LIT, it was almost five thirty. I parked the clunker and went directly to Alex's lab. If there was anything urgent waiting for me in my office, I didn't want to know about it.

Alex abandoned his computer and awarded me a hug and kiss. "So what went on with your day?"

"Let's get to the car. Then I'll relate events in the order in which they occurred."

Once Alex had maneuvered the Mustang out of the lot, I began my narration by telling him that Jim, aided by the Cookie Monster, had resumed his duties.

"I know," said Alex. "If I'd had advance warning, I'd have baked cookies for the tour group. If you tell me when some kids are scheduled, I'll bake."

"Why don't you just bake a bunch and freeze them?"

"I don't think we have enough room in our little freezer."

I thought about that. "Well, why not bake your famous almond meringue cookies. It takes forever before they get stale. If they ever do."

"Because they'll get eaten before they get to the kids."

"Come on, Alex. Who would eat cookies meant for little kids?"

"You."

I had to admit the truth of that.

I then went on to describe the talk I'd had with Jim. "Woof," said Alex, "that poor guy. But doesn't he think his daughter might have noticed that her mother was a nutcake?"

"I don't think he wants to know that. By the way, the kid is coming in to talk with me tomorrow morning. If she seems suitable, we'd like to offer her an internship this summer. Can your Center take her on?"

"Sure," Alex answered, "if she has an interest in what we do. It'd be fun to have an intern to kick around."

Alex pulled into a "scenic view" lay-by. The view wasn't very scenic – just a bunch of farms. We had our snoggle and Alex pulled back on the road. He said, "His name is Fred."

"Whose name is Fred?"

"The Cookie Monster."

"Fred the Cookie Monster," I said. "A cognomen. Like Ivan the Terrible or Ethelred the Unready."

"Those are called cognomens, huh? Like Bush the Beleaguered."

"Cheney the Churl," I offered.

Alex countered with "Perot the Improbable."

"Tony the Tiger," from me.

"That's not fair!" Alex complained.

"Life isn't fair," I pointed out.

Alex pulled off the road, grabbed me, and gave me a smooch. He pulled back on the road, saying "Life is too, fair."

After that intermission, I resumed the narrative, picking up with our introduction to Cabot House and ending with the pop on the schnozz.

"Holy cow!" exclaimed my spouse. "He really hit him?"

"Yep. And Julia immortalized the moment on film."

"What are you gonna do?"

"As soon as I finish with Jim's daughter, I'll brief Pie. My guess is that he'll bring the Secretary's office into it. There is no way that the Committee can function as it is now."

"That sounds right. How about your side of the Committee? Are you happy with it?"

"I couldn't be more pleased. I think Julia is loaded. She's been to Cabot House often – they run an upscale bed and breakfast–and she's going to have her wedding there. That doesn't come cheap."

Alex grinned. "Lots of money, huh? Find out if she'll share."

"We ought to splurge and go to that bed and breakfast some day soon. We've missed our anniversary this year but we should be able to find a good excuse. How about our birthdays this June? They're so close together, it's a natural toofer. We can gorge on breakfast, loll on the front porch, stroll the grounds, maybe go to one of the state parks and hike a little, then come back to Cabot House for dinner."

"Can you make a reservation the next time the Committee meets?"

"*If* it meets, sure."

Alex said, "Don't you think you ought to call Pie tonight? If the Southern Charmer gets in with his cover story first, Pie's liable to get blind-sided."

"I hadn't thought of that, but you're right. I'll call him as soon as we get home."

Last week, I had made Moroccan lentil soup and put it into the freezer for nights like this. Alex microwaved it while I called Pie.

"Hey, *bubele* what's going on?"

Pie yelped when I got the part where Mapledent declared DRA to be the lead agency. "There's no way that *geshvolen goen* is going to get away with that!"

"Wait for the happy ending."

Pie remained quiet until I got to the popped schnozz.

"What??"

"Smacked him right on the nose. Julia, bless her, snapped a picture."

"Do they know you have a photo?"

"Nope. They don't even know we saw the tableau."

Pie laughed. "It'll be fascinating to hear their version of events."

"My guess is that Mapledent will abandon Drumm and try to keep control of the Committee."

Pie said. "You got Jim's kid coming in early tomorrow morning?"

"I do."

"Don't disappoint the kid. I'll call Elaine Ickes – she's the probable incoming Secretary – first thing and see if we can have a phone conversation later in the morning. I'll tell her assistant not to put any calls from DRA through until we've had our conversation. Come to my office as soon as the kid leaves. I want you to be in on the conversation with Elaine." Pie hung up.

By that time the soup was defrosted and ready to eat. Alex had warmed up some French bread and opened the Australian shiraz we had picked up a few days ago.

"What did Pie say?"

"I'm not sure of the Yiddish – I think he called Mapledent a 'puffed-up genius.' He was quite pleased to learn that Julia had a photo of the schnozz affair. He's setting up a conversation with Elaine Ickes tomorrow, after I finish with Jim's daughter. Ickes will probably be our new Secretary. Information not to be repeated."

"My lips are sealed. What if Clinton picks someone else?"

"Then Ickes will brief the new Secretary."

Alex swallowed some soup. "This is really good. With you at the stove and me at the pastry oven we might be able to make a go of our restaurant."

"I'll wait a bit before I quit my day job."

Alex enjoyed the soup for a few more swallows and said, "You know, Pie is a very nice man."

"I know. But what in particular are you referring to?"

Alex answered, "Waiting until you talked with Jim's kid before talking to the Secretary or the incoming Secretary, or whoever he talks to. Most guys would have put a conversation with the Secretary above all else."

I agreed. Pie is a very nice man.

We washed the dishes, put the rest of the soup in the freezer (there should be enough for two more days), and retired to the bedroom. All in all, a satisfactory day.

CHAPTER 4

May 20, 1992

Alex was up, dressed, and assembling the ingredients for waffles when I got out of the shower. I threw on some clothes and was on my way out of the bedroom when I caught a glimpse of myself in the mirror. I looked closer. Had I aged since yesterday?

I went into the kitchen. "Alex, do I look older than I did yesterday?"

"Hmm. C 'mere."

Alex grabbed me and gave me a kiss atop my auburn hair. He held me at arms length. "Your eyes haven't turned gray, yet. They're still green." He patted me on the butt. "If anything, I'd upgrade your fanny from a B+ to A-." I smacked him.

"Cut that out and let me finish the inventory. The bazoom is pretty good. Could be a little bustier but the cleavage is satisfactory."

He buried his face in said cleavage.

I said, "It wouldn't hurt if we were a little late getting to the office."

Half an hour later, Alex resumed assembling the waffle ingredients.

The drive to LIT was uncharacteristically subdued. The weather was weird. A light rain would fall for a while and then the heavens would let loose a torrent and just when I was about to pull off the road until the vision got better, the torrent would subside once more to a light rain. So

41

between my struggles with the precipitation and Alex worrying about whether we would drown, conversation was sporadic.

A few minutes before we reached LIT, the sun suddenly appeared. A signal for communication to begin.

"Bea," said Alex, "do you think you could learn to play a harmonica?"

"A harmonica? Why on earth would I want to play a harmonica?"

"Well," Alex responded, "it's small and it's easy to learn."

"You can say the same thing about a ukulele. Why would I want to learn either instrument?"

"I was thinking," Alex said.

Uh oh.

"I was thinking, not all Gilbert and Sullivan songs have a chorus."

"That is true," I acknowledged.

Alex pulled into a parking slot. "So it would be nice if you could accompany my solos."

He turned off the ignition.

"You goof!" I grabbed his ears and gave him a kiss.

Don knocked on my window. I rolled the window down and stuck my head out.

"You know," Don said, "you keep doing that and his ears will come off."

"You think?" I asked.

"Nah. Not really."

Alex and I got out of the car. Alex trotted off to his lab. Don and I walked to the admin wing.

Don said, "Pie and I were here a little late yesterday. He told me you were going to talk to Jim's kid this morning. Let me know if there's

42

anything I can do."

"Thanks. I can't think of anything right now, but I'll let you know if something comes up. While I'm talking with the kid, pop into Pie's office – he'll tell you about the *contretemps* at my Committee meeting."

I turned toward my office and Don continued toward Pie's place.

Jim and a leggy blonde were waiting at the door to my office. Jim introduced the leggy blonde. "This is my daughter, Chrissie."

We shook hands. "Why are you standing in the corridor? You could have waited in my office. I'm sorry I'm late. It was slow going through the rain. Come on in."

Jim shook his head. "I have a bunch of high school seniors due in half an hour. I'll leave you and Chrissie to it." Jim retreated.

I ushered Chrissie into my office and we both sat down. We looked at one another. Chrissie started to say something and then closed her mouth. It was then my turn to start to say something. What came out was, "Do you know what your Dad wants us to talk about?"

"Not for sure," Chrissie said. "Maybe he thought you'd give me grief counseling or something. But I don't need grief counseling; I'm not grieving. Daddy must have told you what a kook Mom was and he thinks I didn't notice. How could I not notice? She wanted me to become a nun, for pity's sake. Do I look like a nun?"

"Stand up."

Chrissie stood.

I looked her over. She was tall, about five foot eight. Had her dad's blonde hair, which on Chrissie hung straight to her shoulders. Odd colored eyes – gray with green flecks. Full lips. Bosom not too big, not too small. Long legs.

43

"Sit back down, Chrissie."

Chrissie sat.

"On inspection, no. You don't look like a nun."

Chrissie burst out laughing. "I don't believe you said that!"

"Believe it. If you don't want to be a nun, what do you want to do?"

"Right now, I want to get an education."

"What courses are you taking?"

"Molecules and Cells. Statistics. Literature and Society. Biological Anthropology. And, of course, the dreaded phys ed."

"That's an impressive load for a sophomore."

"Well, yeah, but I came in with a lot of advance placement credits so I can take more electives than most sophomores. And I really do want to get an education. I only *look* like an airhead."

I laughed. "You don't look like an airhead any more than you look like a nun. What phys ed are you taking?

"Karate."

"Karate? Why karate?"

"Because karate and golf were the only things offered when I had a free hour."

"I see your point."

"Actually, I'm pretty good at it. I have a brown belt. The course will be over before I get a black, though."

"Well, I'm sure even a brown belt will be more useful than golf."

"Absolutely. If I'm ever in a dark alley and get accosted by a pine board, I'll smack that sucker in two."

I think this kid takes after her father.

"From your course load, it looks like you might be leaning toward the biological sciences.   Is that right?"

"Yeah.   Eventually, I'd really like to get a doctorate in horticulture."

"Why horticulture?"

"Well, this might sound stupid, but I'd like to create something beautiful.   Horticulturists do a lot of hybridization and if they know what they're doing, truly beautiful things can come out of it.   But before you can really know what you're doing, you have to learn a lot of different fields – that's why I'm taking Molecules and Cells.   I don't know if that will ever be useful, but it might be.

"I can paint reasonably well, and draw a little bit better, but I'll never be a great artist.   So one of the ways I might be able to create something beautiful is to be a horticulturist. Does that sound dumb?"

"No.   It sounds eminently sensible."

"The thing is," Chrissie continued, "I'm only a sophomore and I'm sure that I want to be a horticulturist of some sort.   But by the time I'm ready to commit, I may not be that infatuated with ornamentals. Vegetables and fruit trees have their charms. When you look at the courses you have to take, it's almost like going to a med. school for plants – you need plant physiology and plant pathology, genetics, biochemistry...."

Chrissie suddenly burst into tears. I got up and put my arms around her.   She sobbed for a bit.   Then, "She didn't used to be so weird.   She was a wonderful Mom until I was about ten and then she just got weirder and weirder."

Chrissie looked up at me.   "Am I going to get weird, do you think?"

I hugged her.   "I doubt it, Chrissie.   But if you come see me once a month, I'll do a thorough inspection and tell you if you're getting weird."

Chrissie wiped her nose with the back of her hand. "You're all heart, Dr. Goode.

"Are you going to have kids? You'd make a great Mom."

This was not a place I wanted to go. "No. I can't have children. Result of an auto accident."

Chrissie looked stricken. "Geez, I'm sorry Dr. Goode. I shouldn't have asked that."

I kissed the top of her head. "Not to worry. Come on, let's go to the ladies room and clean up the tears."

We mopped up the ravages and returned to my office.

"Did your dad tell you that we have a Biology Center?"

"He did."

"Did he tell you that we have a resident horticulturist?"

"You do? I don't think Daddy knows that. But why does LIT have a horticulturist on staff?"

"Those beautiful hybrids you talked about have quite a bit of commercial value. Not to mention the fruit and vegetables. Industry relies on us to help produce hybrids. We're hoping that one of these days those hybrids will add to our list of exports.

"If you like, I'll call over to the Biology Lab and see if someone can show you around."

"That would be great!"

I dialed Molly Cameron (no relation to the Jeanne Cameron on my staff), Alex's counterpart in the Biology Center.

"Cameron."

"Hey Molly, this is Bea. I've got Jim Daley's daughter in my office. She's a sophomore at UMD, interested in biology in general and advanced horticulture in particular. Is there someone in the lab who has

46

time to show her around?"

"For Jim's kid? I'll do it myself. Bring her down."

"We're on our way."

I stood up. "Let's go, Chrissie."

Molly Cameron is a formidable woman. In her late fifties, she's about my five foot four in height, with silver hair, cut short in back, a bit longer in front and swept across her forehead to one side. She is solidly built. Molly is a serious, no-nonsense person. She runs her lab with a steel fist – doesn't bother with a velvet glove – and takes no prisoners. She demands perfection and she gets it. For reasons that I have never been able to discern, despite her demanding character, her staff loves her. Come to think of it, so do I. Go figure.

I walked Chrissie down to Molly's lab, introduced her, and went to see if it was time to talk with Elaine.

Don was still in Pie's office when I got there. "That bozo really smacked him on the honker, huh?"

"That he did." I turned to Pie. "When do we call Elaine?"

"We don't. She's going to call us. Anytime this morning after ten. I guessed your interview with Jim's kid would be over by then. How did it go?"

"Very well. Chrissie's a great kid. Very smart. Sense of humor. Knows where she's going. And extremely good looking."

"When do I get to meet her?" Don asked.

"She also has a karate brown belt."

"Damn!" Don said.

We laughed. "She's interested in all things biological, so I took her to the Biology Center. Molly offered to show her around. I'll check with Molly later. She usually won't take undergrads, but she might be persuaded to take Chrissie on as an intern. She really is an impressive kid."

"Don't lean on Molly," Pie said. "She may have someone else in mind."

"Molly, being Molly, will not do anything she doesn't want to do."

The intercom came alive. Lenore informed us that Ms. Ickes was on the line.

Pie picked up. "Hello, Elaine. I'm going to put this on speaker. Bea is here and she can give you the story better than I can."

"Hello, Bea. What's going on?"

"Good morning, Ma'am..."

"Call me Elaine."

"Good morning, Elaine. It was an interesting meeting. We no sooner got into the room than G. Douglas Mapledent announced that because DRA was the lead agency, he would chair the committee."

"He announced *what*?"

"He announced that DRA was the lead agency," I answered.

"Did you let him get away with that crap?"

"I didn't respond one way or the other. I was afraid that if I challenged him, I might get you into an inter-agency war."

Silence on the other end of the phone. Then, "Good call. I'll get this fixed without bloodshed."

Pie cut in. "Wait, don't hang up. The best is yet to come."

"That isn't enough?"

"No," I said, "that's the least of it. Julia took Billy and me on a guided tour of the grounds and around the wetland. We heard some shouting and rounded a bend to find two of the DRA team. One of the guys had just punched the other one in the nose."

"You're kidding."

"Nope. Julia took a picture of it. Drumm with fists clenched. Farrington holding his nose."

"Oh, my God. What happened then?"

"I signaled Julia and Billy to keep quiet and we tip-toed back to Cabot House."

"So nobody knows you saw and recorded the, uh, event?"

"That's right. When we made our scheduled return to the meeting, G. Douglas regretted that he had to cut the meeting short – some very important foreign visitors had unexpectedly arrived at DRA, and the DRA team was urgently needed at headquarters."

Elaine laughed. "Well, lame as it is, that's probably the best story he could dream up without the help of a blue-ribbon committee. What do you want to happen?"

"I'd like to resume being Committee chair..."

"Done."

"I'd like Drumm off the Committee for certain and G. Douglas off if possible."

"Drumm will certainly come off. I can't really dictate who should be on the DRA team unless the member in question is violent. But I doubt if Mapledent will want to stay on even if the current DRA Secretary or Roger, for some strange reason, allows it."

I looked questioningly at Pie.

He whispered, "Roger Biddle. Presumed incoming Secretary of DRA."

Elaine continued. "I'll call Roger right now and get back to you as soon as he gets this resolved with the current Secretary."

She rang off.

Pie and Don were both grinning. Pie remarked, "I almost feel sorry for that poor *schmuck* Mapledent. Almost.

"Let's go get an early lunch. I want to be back in my office when Elaine calls."

We picked up our lunches in the cafeteria and were happily chewing over the conversation with Elaine when Molly Cameron walked up.

"That's some kid Jim's got," she said.

I looked at Pie, who nodded. I said to Molly, "I know you only take graduate students, but would you consider offering Chrissie a summer internship?"

Molly looked smug. "She accepted our offer before she left the building. Jim's so proud of her I thought he'd do a cartwheel."

Pie said, "Knowing Jim, I bet he did one as soon as you left."

Don asked Molly, "You think the kid's that good?"

"Damn right. She spent a lot of the time in the lab discussing hybridization with Ralph. He'd like to mentor her until she gets her undergraduate degree. He says then she can mentor him."

Molly went on her way.

Don leaned back. "It's nice when things work out the way you hoped."

We returned to our respective offices. I waded through the accumulation of paperwork, stopping occasionally to congratulate myself on introducing Chrissie to the Biology Center.

Around two o'clock Lenore called to say that Ms. Ickes was on the phone with Pie. I beat it to his office.

"Here she is," Pie said into the phone. Then to me, "We waited for you before we got to business." He activated the speaker.

"Pretty good news," Elaine said. "There is no question but that Bea leads the Committee. Drumm is on administrative leave while he takes an anger management course. And Mapledent is, what one might call, 'unexpected'. The DRA Secretary suggested that he leave the Committee and Mapledent expressed a deep desire to stay on it. The Secretary gave in under the condition that if he got any complaint about Mapledent's behavior, he was outta there."

I was surprised, to say the least. "Why on earth does he want to stay on?'

"Mapledent thinks that he has expertise that would be, and I quote, 'of inestimable value to the Committee.' Can you live with that?"

"Sure. As long as he behaves himself he may very well be of value. What did he say about the brawl?"

Elaine giggled. Actually giggled. "He explained to the Secretary that Farrington had been standing outside a door and someone had opened the door and hit him in the nose. Also that Drumm had asked to be removed from the Committee because of his workload.

"The Secretary then told the idiot that he appreciated his efforts to protect his colleagues, but that DoTI not only saw Drumm hit Farrington but took a picture of it. They then spent the rest of the conversation trying to figure out how they might prevent Farrington from suing."

"And what conclusion did they reach?" Pie asked.

"They're going to try to bribe him with a promotion to GS-15. The Secretary can bull it through Human Resources, but they don't know if he'll take it.

"Oh, and Mapledent will appoint a qualified woman to take

Drumm's place on the Committee."

Pie said, "Thank you, Elaine, we appreciate this."

I added my thanks.

Elaine said, "Don't mention it. This is the most fun I've had since I said I'd take the crazy job." She hung up.

"We'd better tell 'to whom it may concern,'" Pie said. "I'll tell Don."

"I'll tell Julia and Billy."

I asked Lenore to set up a conference call with my Committee members and returned to my office. Shortly, I had the two of them on the line. Billy especially was delighted with the current state of affairs.

"Gee," he said, "Mapledent is still on the committee, huh? That should be fun."

"Billy," I said, "behave yourself."

"Spoilsport," he said.

And with that we parted.

I walked to Jim's office to congratulate him on the raising of his wonderful kid. He looked a little sheepish.

"She already knew how nutty her mother was, huh?"

"She could hardly miss it. The woman wanted her to be a nun."

"Chrissie? A nun? Oh, for pete's sake."

"She might have looked good in a wimple. If she could find an Order that still wore wimples."

That earned me an eye-roll.

"Thanks for everything, Bea. Chrissie is thrilled about the internship."

"I had nothing to do with the internship. I was going to suggest it to Molly, but she beat me to it."

"Honest?"

"Yeah. I was having lunch with Pie and Don. Molly stopped at our table and told us that the Center, particularly the horticulturist, wanted her there."

"How about that!"

Jim's grin didn't stop until it got to his ears. I waited for the cartwheel. When it wasn't forthcoming, I bade the man farewell and went to tell my husband that I was ready to head home if he was.

The weather had cleared and the evening drive was less terrifying than the morning one.

"I took a peek at Jim's schedule. He has fifth graders coming in tomorrow afternoon."

"Good. I'll bake cookies tonight."

"Please make enough for LIT's senior management."

"I could make enough for the seventh airborne fleet and it wouldn't be enough for you guys. Particularly if you count Lenore in. But I'll make an effort."

I pulled in to the scenic lay-by and we had a satisfactory snoggle before continuing the journey.

"How did your conversation with Ickes go?"

"Couldn't have gone much better. Drumm's on administrative leave and has to take an anger management course. For some reason, G. Douglas wants to stay on the Committee. The DRA Secretary is going to let him stay as long as we don't have any more complaints about him."

"Geez," Alex said, "I'da thought he would disappear after getting humiliated."

"Apparently he thinks we can't get along without him."

Alex shrugged.

"How'd you like Jim's kid?"

I laughed. "You're off the hook. She's not a computernik. She's interested in things biological, so I took her to Molly's lab. They offered her a summer internship."

"Molly did? That kid must be something. Molly doesn't suffer fools or undergrads gladly."

"The kid *is* something."

We stopped at the corner market to get the makings of the cookies, drove home, and ate the second installment of the Moroccan lentil soup. Alex assumed his role of Baker-in-Chief while I did the dishes.

CHAPTER 5

May 21, 1992

Alex loaded the cookies into four separate bags: a big bag for the visiting kids, another big bag for his Center, a smaller bag for the Management staff, and a separate little bag for Lenore.

We put the bags in the trunk and arranged ourselves in the front seat of the Mustang. "Maybe," I said, "you should make cookies for the Bio Center, too."

Alex extracted the car from its parking place and headed down the street. Once he got things running smoothly, he gave me a look. "If Molly Cameron wants to feed her brood, she can learn to bake!"

"I thought you liked Molly."

"I do like Molly," Alex said. "I like lots of people. I like Bill Clinton. But I'm not going to bake for his entourage. He can do his own baking."

I pondered an image of a 1950s retro Bill Clinton, dolled up as Betty Furness, opening an oven door and intoning, "You can be sure, if it's The White House." Maybe he could adopt it as the slogan for his second term campaign. 'The Economy, Stupid' should have run its course by then.

Alex and I spent the next half hour adding furbelows to the image. Bill Clinton burning his fingers. Bill Clinton tasting a cookie and gagging. Bill Clinton setting the kitchen on fire. The possibilities were endless.

We turned onto the winding road and proceeded to butcher "John

Wellington Wells" as we traveled toward LIT. In the absence of harmonica accompaniment, I caroled doo-wah in the background.

My phone was ringing as I reached my office. I picked up. It was Chrissie.

"Dr. Goode, I just wanted to thank you for setting me up with the Bio Center..."

I tried to interrupt to tell her that I hadn't done any setting up – just introducing. But Chrissie had acquired a full head of steam.

"...and Dr. Cameron was just wonderful. She showed me all the equipment, did you know they have a spectrophonometer and a ph meter, and equipment for high-speed liquid chromatography and I can't remember it all offhand and Ralph, that's Dr. Hamilton, wants to mentor me and everyone in the Lab is very supportive and I'm going to learn an amazing amount of things. So I just wanted to call and thank you."

"You're welcome, Chrissie."

"I love you, Dr. Goode." Chrissie hung up.

I sat looking at the receiver for a minute. Then I hung up.

I took two cookies from the Management bag and put them in my top desk drawer. I re-sealed the bag and took it and Lenore's bag toward Pie's place. I gave the little bag to Lenore. "Alex baked these for you."

"Oh, thank you, Bea. But I'm on a diet. I'll give them to someone else."

As I walked toward the office, I heard Lenore opening her bag, and the subsequent crunch of Lenore's teeth destroying a cookie.

Don was already there. I signaled the presence of Alex's cookies and passed the bag around. Don frowned at the bag. "Did you remove a couple for your own use later?"

"I cannot tell a lie...."

"Yes, you can if you don't think you'll get caught. You're as bad as Lenore," Don said.

"No I'm not. I don't pretend I'm on a diet."

"Okay," said Pie, "you're only almost as bad as Lenore. You're both *chazzers*."

Pie took a big handful of cookies. I forbore to comment.

We spent the greater part of the morning discussing the following week's to-do list. Aside from the preparation for and attendance at the Committee meetings, I was delegated to get summaries of the important trade data from Ben and to prepare a briefing on same for Pie. He was due to meet with the Louisiana Congressional delegation. I had a leg up on the assignment since I had already asked Ben for the Fisheries data. Gulf of Mexico shrimp ranked as a major export for Louisiana. The news would not be good for the delegation. More and more shrimp are being imported each year. Less and less are being exported. Bummer.

We broke for lunch around noon. Lenore stopped me as I approached her desk. "Bea, what's the difference between global warming and climate change?"

"Global warming causes climate change."

"Like if I get a nail in my tire it causes it to go flat?"

"Exactly."

"Oh. Thank you."

On the way back to my office I pondered the change in Lenore since Pie became Director. Under the old regime, she was as much the misogynist as G. Douglas. She would not have approved of women such as me mingling in the upper reaches of Management. Never would she have asked me a substantive question. What a difference Pie had made!

I picked up Julia and Billy and we headed off to Cabot House. The clunker behaved itself reasonably well. It stalled at red lights but usually restarted before the driver in the car behind us got hysterical.

Julia had developed the photo of The Fight. I examined it at the first red light. Julia was a fine photographer, among her other talents. The picture was sharp, the composition magnificent. Drumm looked menacing. Farrington appeared grievously wounded. In response to my plea, Julia agreed to make me a copy suitable for framing.

That settled, I gave my passengers the results of the deliberations of the gaggle of Secretaries and presumptive Secretaries.

"I wonder who the 'qualified woman' will be," Julia mused. "They don't have many senior women at DRA, but they do have four or five in our field who are pretty good. We can work well with any of them.

"One of the women, in particular – Marcy Grossman – would be a good match for the Committee. She's an ecologist by training but has had a lot of experience with science policy. She can be a little prickly, but if we had a vacant slot I'd like to get her over to DoTI.

"Bea, could you make the time to have lunch with Marcy and me – just to see what you think?"

"Sure, but even if DoTI had an open slot, my opinion wouldn't be worth much. Unless the slot were at LIT and even then, Molly Cameron is a law unto herself."

Julia nodded and went on to describe the other few 'pretty good' women.

In the event, Mapledent chose none of them.

The three DRA members were just settling into their chairs when we arrived. In addition to Mapledent and Farrington, there was a young, skinny woman with light brown hair, an enviable complexion, and no make-up whatever. She was wearing a frilly, puffed-sleeve blouse, and a flowered skirt that ended about four inches below her knees. She sat down before I could see her shoes. I bet myself that they were brown oxfords.

We settled ourselves and I welcomed everyone. Mapledent gave me a saccharine smile. "Well, well, little lady. I see you have friends in high places."

I gave him a somewhat more sincere smile. Sugar, not saccharine. "Yes, as it happens, I do."

Billy entered the discussion. "In the circumstances, Doug, I think 'big momma' would be a more accurate sobriquet than 'little lady.'"

Doug acknowledged the comment with a nod. "Thank you. I will be mindful of the correction."

I cut that discussion short. "Doug, would you introduce our new member?"

"Yes, of course. This is Emmaline Stutz, our ecologist. I'm sure she will be a productive addition to the Committee."

We three DoTI members introduced ourselves to Emmaline.

I then asked Billy to take minutes and he began rooting around in his briefcase for a pad of paper. Julia handed him one. He found his own pen.

"Before you begin," Doug said, "I forgot my briefcase in my sitting room. I'd like to have it before we start."

He turned to Emmaline. "Honey, would you get my briefcase, please." Emmaline beetled out of the room before we could say anything. She was wearing brown oxfords.

While she was gone, Doug asked me, "Did you enjoy your tour of the grounds?"

"Enormously," I answered. "Fortunately, we didn't encounter any crawling reptiles."

"Don't tell me you're afraid of snakes." Doug shook his head.

I smiled. "Only the crawling kind."

Julia and Billy managed not to laugh.

When Emmaline returned with the briefcase, I took up the first item on my agenda. "Doug, I would like you to retire to your sitting room and write a first draft of our Mission statement. Take your time with it. As you pointed out last time, this is our first order of business and extremely important. Please have six legible copies of it by four thirty and we will review it before we leave."

Mapledent looked at me suspiciously but he stood up. "I'm sure you won't mind if I take Emmaline with me."

Emmaline stood up.

"I do mind, Doug. It's important that our new member becomes integrated with the group as soon as possible."

Mapledent picked up his briefcase and stormed out of the room. The door slammed behind him.

I turned to Emmaline. "Tell us a bit about yourself. Where did you go to school?"

Emmaline bit her lip. "I don't think you should have done that, Dr. Goode. Dr. Mapledent is very angry."

Julia smiled confidingly. "That's all right, Emmaline. None of us gives a rat's ass about Doug's moods."

Emmaline looked shocked. Farrington grinned. Billy punched the air. And I nearly choked trying to stifle a guffaw.

In the silence, a Cabot House staff member entered and took orders for drinks. I asked him to stop in Mapledent's room and get his order also.   The staff member nodded and departed.

I started again.   "Emmaline, where did you go to school?"

"I graduated from Beeglebush University last year."

We all looked at her.   "It's a small Virginia school.   We have close ties to the Baptists."

I said.   "And you majored in ecology and came to work for DRA?"

"Yes, ma'am."

"And you report to Dr. Mapledent?"

"Well, not directly.   I'm only a GS-9 so I don't directly report to someone as high up as Dr. Mapledent."

"Yes.   Of course.   Well, I'm sure you will be a real asset to the Committee."

We'd have been much better off with Chrissie the Undergrad.

We then took up the first real item of business.   Should the work be done in-house or by contractors?   This was at the top of the agenda, not because it was most important, but because – no matter where it would be done – it was essential to get the working team on board as early as possible.   If in-house there had to be time to reassign personnel.   If by contractors, a request for proposal had to be written, issued, evaluated, and awarded before the real work could start.

The discussion was sensible and collegial, for the most part. Howie Farrington turned out to be a first-rate member. He was one of those people able to disagree without being confrontational. He would work out well.   Emmaline, on the other hand, just sat there once we assured her that the Committee's work would not have anything to do with Evolution. Sometime during the discussion, a Cabot House staff member wheeled in pastries, coffee, and Julia's tea.

Once we decided that we didn't have sufficient in-house resources but needed contractors, we narrowed it down to universities. There would be too much political detritus if we went to the private sector. Next question – who would write and issue the request for proposal? Since this was an administrative matter, I took the assignment.

At four o'clock G. Douglas joined us. I apprised him of the decisions to date.

"Well," he said, "I hope we won't be forced to include any HBCUs* in the group that receives the Request."

"What would be your objection?" I asked.

"They just aren't up to standards. I'm not opposed to Negroes in general, but they just aren't good schools."

"I think that both Tuskegee and Fisk have first-rate Biology Departments, and Tuskegee offers a solid degree program in Agriculture," Howie said.

"Now look," Mapledent responded, "Some of my best friends..."

"That's enough," I said. "Step out of the room with me, Doug. Julia, please assume the chair while I'm away."

Doug and I left the room and closed the door behind us.

I glared at him. "I am not interested in the size, shape, or color of your friends, assuming that you have any. But you will not bring racist crap into this meeting. Is that understood?"

"Now, Bea, I was not being racist, I was just being realistic."

"Go tell that on the mountain. Meanwhile, for the duration of this discussion, shut up."

Mapledent turned on his heel and returned to the room.

I began to follow him and noticed Dexter Hamilton standing

---

* Historically Black Colleges and Universities

against the wall. "Way to go, Dr. Goode," he whispered.

I re-joined the meeting. Julia looked relieved to see me.

By now it was four thirty and time to look at Mapledent's Mission statement. He circulated the copies.

Mission statement

The Committee is responsible for providing leadership in the establishment and maintenance of criteria after due deliberation that will be used in the determination of the   real or perceived notion of climate change, the likelihood in fact of mans' significant influence or effect on global warming, and after such determination, the acquisition of knowledge of mans' preventative measures or actions that should be recommended to lessen such effects. Content managers, led by the Chairman, shall establish and administer a process in the determination of such criteria and shall develop templates, per chapter II, section (9)(a)(12) of the Precept Manual, that will allow a scientifically expert level of understanding of the current research about global climate change.   Peer reviewed research shall be used in the general interpretation of the nature and influence of man on climate, and potential preventative measures.

The Chairman shall convene and deliberate over the team of content managers and meet regularly to better understand the science and issues and create appropriate documents.   The Chairman shall make the final recommendation to the Secretaries of the Department of Rural Affairs and the Department of Trade and Industry and shall ensure all materials are appropriately organized and archived.

We sat there, stunned.

Finally, Billy said, "Is there a mission buried in there?"

"You must understand that this is just a First Draft," Mapledent said.   "Please do not hesitate to, uh, tweak the document."

"Well," Emmaline said.

Emmaline speaks?

"I think that's a perfectly wonderful statement just as it is."

"You gotta be kid..." Billy sputtered.   I kicked him.

"Ouch," Billy said and said no more.

"Yes, Emmaline," I said.   "It certainly is thorough.   Now, everybody please take it with you, read through it and if you have any, uh, tweaking, bring your comments the next time we convene.   Next Tuesday at two o'clock?"

Nods all around.   Meeting adjourned.

Predictably, Billy exploded as soon as we got in the car.   "That guy's gotta go.   Aside from the fact the he's a racist moron, how could he bring that little kid into the meeting?   Didn't he have to clear it with his Secretary?"

"The DRA Secretary," I said, "will leave his post before January, whether Bush wins or loses.   He had an agenda when he came in and he'll be trying to get it completed before he goes out.   He's not going to waste time on Mapledent's appointments to an obscure committee."

"It's not an 'obscure committee,' Julia objected.   "It's a priority of the incoming Administration."

"But not of the outgoing Administration.   I doubt if the DRA Secretary even looked at the appointment.   Just signed off on it. Or had his secretary sign off for him."

"Shit," said Billy. "And what are you going to do about that ridiculous Mission statement."

"Nothing.   My intent is to keep G. Douglas sequestered, writing nonsense, while the rest of us get on with the real job.   The problem is the Stutz kid.   She might become a drag on the Committee but I don't want to let Mapledent take her to run his errands."

"Why not?" Julia asked.

"Because my spies reported that he has a case of roving hands. We can't leave that kid alone in a room with him.   We'll just have to deal with her on the Committee."

I dropped Julia and Billy off at the DoTI building and headed to LIT.   Before I announced my presence to Alex, I ate my two cookies.

CHAPTER 6
May 22–25, 1992

"This is the Memorial Day weekend," I reminded Alex. "Busy time for the alpacas. The Cokers are going to shear them on Saturday. Claudia said that it should take the better part of the day."

"Cool," Alex said. "Will they let us help?"

"From what Claudia said, they'll need all the help they can get."

We threw some extra clothes into our backpacks, deposited the backpacks in the trunk, and headed toward LIT.

Leaving the Washington area on the Friday before Memorial day was no joy. My foot was on the brake more than on the accelerator and by the time we reached the turn-off, I was a thoroughly disgruntled woman.

The winding road to LIT, however, was reasonably free of traffic, the sun was shining, and I pulled off the road to let the top down. I was no longer disgruntled. In celebration, once on the road, Alex began to warble.

Alex: I have a song to sing, O!

Me: Sing me your song, O

Alex: It is sung to the moon by a love-lorn loon

Who fled from the mocking throng-o

It's the song of a merry man moping mum

We stopped at one of the few traffic lights on the road. A car stopped behind us as Alex continued:

Whose soul was sad and whose glance was glum

The guy in the car behind us stuck his head out of his window,

"Hey, pipe down. I liked it better when I was driving on the effing highway."

The light turned green and, with no one coming in the opposite direction, I waved the car around us.

When he was a safe distance away, Alex continued,

> Who sipped no sup and who craved no crumb
>
> As he sighed for the love of a lady
>
> Me: Hey-di, hey-di, misery me, lack-a day-di
>
> He sipped no sup and he craved no crumb
>
> As he sighed for the love of a lady.

Alex turned to me. "Are you sure you don't want to take up the harmonica?"

"Hah!" I snorted. "It wasn't _me_ that the guy was complaining about."

We rode a few miles in sullen silence. Finally, Alex said "Pull into the lay-by."

I did. I removed my seatbelt and settled in for a satisfying snoggle. I pulled back on the road and Alex said, "I really love you..."

"I love you too," I said.

"...even if you don't sound as good as a harmonica."

I couldn't help it. I laughed.

There was a note on my desk. "Come to Pie's office as soon as you arrive."

Pie and Don looked grim. "Sit down," Pie said. "Elaine wants a word with you." He pressed the intercom and asked Lenore to let Elaine know that we were ready.

"What's going on?" I asked.

"You'll find out in a minute," Don answered.

The phone crackled. Elaine said, "Bea, what the hell do you think you're doing? Are you trying to start a war with DRA?"

I made the only sensible comment I could think of. "Huh?"

Elaine continued. "Dr. Mapledent complained that you refused to allow him to express an opinion. I realize that the man is not the loveliest flower in the greenhouse, but he is entitled to participate in the workings of the Committee."

"Oh, for heaven's sake. Did that jackass mention what opinion I stifled?"

"Not that I know of," Elaine admitted.

"We were discussing possible contractors and had decided that Universities were the best choice. G. Douglas then objected to any HBCU being included in the mix. When he got to the part 'Some of my best friends are Negroes' I took him out of the room and told him to keep his racist garbage out of the meeting and to shut up until the discussion was concluded."

Pie and Don had stopped looking grim.

There was silence on the other end of the line. Then, "I apologize. I should have known better. I don't suppose anyone overheard that conversation."

"As a matter of fact, someone did. Neither of us realized that the Cabot House manager was standing in the shadows. I noticed him when I turned to follow Mapledent back into the room."

"Dexter Hamilton overheard you? He's a good friend of mine. Did he say anything?"

"Yes, he certainly did. He said, 'Way to go, Dr. Goode.'"

Elaine was thoughtful. "I'll get to Roger right now."

She chortled. "No way could Mapledent have known that his next Secretary is Black. He's in for a shock when the Administration changes. I apologize again, Bea. I wasn't thinking straight." She hung up.

I looked at Pie and Don. They looked at one another. "O kay," said Pie, "we apologize too."

"So buy me lunch."

"Are you going to order dessert?" Don asked.

"Damn straight!" And with that I swept out of the office.

I stopped at Ben's and picked up the trade statistics. Louisiana has quite a bit going for it. Petroleum and petroleum refining, natural gas, sugar cane, rice, pecans, and cotton. The state provides about a quarter of the seafood consumed in the U.S. But the chances were good that the delegation wanted to talk to Pie about shrimp. Once upon a time we exported much shrimp. Now we *import* about two and a half billion dollars worth as opposed to about a half million in exports. The shrimp fishers and processors are dying an economic death. Much of the imports are coming from southeast Asia – Thailand in particular. And those countries are subsidizing their shrimpers to a fare-thee-well. W e can't compete. The Louisianans are going to plump for punitive tariffs or counter-subsidies. The international ramifications of either course are beyond this poor bureaucrat's ken. Pie's in for a rough session.

I wrote up the briefing notes and brought them to the typing pool.

Lunch with Pie and Don was particularly enjoyable. I don't usually get a salad, but this time I got one. Meatloaf is my favorite cafeteria main course, but the roast beef is more expensive. I got that. Also bread. Two pats of butter. I finished with rhubarb crumble and a tall iced tea.

Don, a notorious cheapskate, watched in mounting horror as I filled up my tray. We found a table and sat down. I really didn't want to eat all that, but no matter my discomfort – *those guys would pay.*

We had no sooner arranged our napkins when Ralph Hamilton, the Bio Center's horticulturist strolled by. I hailed him.

Ralph is a coffee colored man whose voice retains its West Indian lilt despite forty years on the mainland. He's a real sweetie.

"Ralph, thank you for taking Chrissie on."

"The pleasure is all mine." He looked at my tray. "Didn't you notice that today's soup is mulligatawny?"

"No, I didn't. Thanks for the alert. I'll get some."

Don said, "Aren't you putting on a little weight, Bea?"

Pie stifled a laugh.

"No, actually I've lost a pound or two."

Pie said, "Give it up, Don. I'll flip you to see which of us gets her the soup."

They flipped. Don went off to get the soup. Insult to injury.

Ralph looked mystified, but remaining unenlightened, bade us good-bye, and trundled off to join his fellow biologists.

I turned to Pie. "I've been wondering, how did Elaine get involved in the latest Mapledent brouhaha? I thought her probable appointment was a closely held secret. I haven't seen her name mentioned in any of the newspaper speculations."

"It *is* a secret," he answered. "What happened was that Mapledent went around his chain of command and called the DRA Secretary's office directly. The gatekeeper decided that the Secretary had suffered quite enough of that *shmegegge* and palmed the *kvetch* off on the DoTI

Secretary. He is both my and Elaine's friend, so he gave me a heads up and asked Elaine to handle it."

Don returned with my soup. He set it in front of me with ill grace. I took a spoonful of soup. It was quite tasty.

Continuing the conversation, I said, "I'm surprised they've been able to keep it secret – these things usually leak within minutes."

Don looked puzzled; I clued him in. "We're talking about Elaine's upcoming appointment."

"The only people who know," Pie said, "are us, Clinton himself, Roger Biddle, Elaine, and Elaine's executive secretary at IBM. Neither Clinton nor Elaine nor Roger are talking, we're not talking, and if Elaine's executive secretary didn't know how to keep her mouth shut, she wouldn't be Elaine's executive secretary."

I left my two colleagues to divvy up my lunch expenses and returned to my office, where I found a 'please call' message from Julia.

Wondering what that was about, I returned the call.

"Can you break for a cup of coffee with Marcy and me later this afternoon? If we come up to your joint?"

"Sure. What's going on?"

There was an audible sigh from Julia. "The poor woman is beside herself. She wanted that place on the Committee, for which she is eminently qualified, and Mapledent first appointed Drumm, which wasn't so bad, at least he's well trained. But then he brought in that silly kid. Marcy needs to meet a senior woman who hasn't been trod upon."

"I confess," I said. "I qualify. Three o'clock okay? In my office and then to the cafeteria for coffee."

"Sounds good." Julia rang off.

I did my best not to goggle when the two of them arrived. The diminutive Julia was leading an Amazon – maybe six feet tall and built like a brick outhouse. Marcy Grossman certainly made an impression.

We walked to the cafeteria, got some coffee, and grabbed a table in the corner. I smiled at Julia. "No tea?"

She grinned. "The stuff they have in the cafeterias is not recognizably tea. The stuff in my cup is barely recognizable as coffee. But I'll drink it anyway – as penance."

"Penance for what?" I asked.

"Thinking evil thoughts about G. Douglas." She took a sip of the brown liquid. "I wanted you and Marcy to meet – I think you'll like one another."

I turned to the Amazon. Man, she was big. Not just tall, she must have been four feet wide from her shoulders all the way to her hips. "These are exciting times for ecologists," I said. "Global warming must be stirring up the relationships between the environment and those of us, large and small, that live in it."

"You better believe it," Marcy said. She had an extremely pleasant voice. "I'm just pissed that Mapledent won't let me contribute where I can be of the most help."

"He is a trial," I sympathized. "But he doesn't control the only place where your expertise might come in handy. The Ecological Society just put up a committee to deal with endangered species."

Marcy snorted. "Being on that committee wouldn't help my career any. Besides, I don't think women should do all that much volunteering. It's just another place where we get exploited. We should get paid for what we do."

I glanced over at Julia, who looked bewildered. "But Marcy," she said, "all of the men on the committee are volunteers."

"Yeah, but they've already got their place in the market. They aren't going to move over for the likes of me.

"Just look what Mapledent did to me. How many briefings did I write that he signed and took credit for? Fifty? A hundred? And when reward time came along he gave the honor to that toadying, sniveling Jesus freak who wouldn't know an ecological crisis if it swallowed her."

I took it that Marcy was somewhat upset.

She drank some coffee and calmed down a bit.

"Here," she handed me some papers. "Could you look at these?"

It was her resume. Bachelors degree from Colorado State. Specialized in wetlands management. Series of increasingly important DRA field positions. Then hit a snag when she moved to headquarters where she stalled out at GS-13.

"Is there any chance that I might transfer to LIT if and when there's an opening?"

I shook my head. "I doubt it. We're a research organization. Except in management, we only hire PhD's or people who have extensive and impressive research publications."

"And how many of your senior managers are women?"

I answered, "If by senior managers you mean SES positions, there are five altogether – three of us in the Director's office and two Center directors. Of the five, two of us are women."

I wouldn't say that Marcy sneered. But she came close. "And one of the two women is a close friend of the Director."

Julia gasped.

"Hold it a minute, Marcy," I said. Not everything is a conspiracy – although working for Mapledent might make it seem so. The Director had nothing to do with my ascension to the SES ranks. I was a GS-15 when he joined LIT and my promotion was suggested and pushed by Don Cromarty, my boss at the time. It might also be of interest to you that of the five senior executives at LIT, four of us have PhDs."

"Everyone except you?" Marcy asked.

"Everyone except Don," I answered.

I stood up and returned her resume. "Thank you for coming. It's been a pleasure."

Alex's and my weekend retreat is a log cabin on an alpaca farm, located on the winding road between Washington and LIT. We pass it whenever we go to work and one day we observed the alpacas grazing in the field near the fence. We pulled over and made their acquaintance. The next time we drove up, we pulled over and fed them some apples. This went on for a bit. Eventually the alpacas began to expect us and would come to the fence to exact their apple toll as soon as they heard us arrive. The herd was benignly presided over by a couple of llamas. The llamas were courteous enough, but somewhat stand-offish.

The farm's owner, Daryl Coker, noticed us and one day he approached, introduced himself, and told us a bit about his critters. They are very cute, very shaggy animals – weigh one hundred fifty pounds top. They are guarded by two four hundred pound llamas, who are very protective of their charges. The llamas are very dignified. The alpacas are adorable. In some ways, their temperament is similar to that of a cat. Like cats, they are both shy and intensely curious. If you just stand in their vicinity, eventually they'll come over to get a closer look at you. Their coat produces wonderful, warm, soft fiber. Much warmer and softer than sheep fleece. The llamas also produce fiber, a great deal coarser than that of either sheep or alpacas. It's great for mats or wall hangings.

One day, Daryl came to us with a proposition. He had a log cabin on the property which had been inhabited by his son and daughter-in-law. When they had saved enough money to buy a place of their own, they moved out and the cabin had been uninhabited ever since. The Cokers didn't like that, so they offered it to us if we would maintain it in its current excellent condition and pay the utility bills. It was a deal.

Because of our weekend residency, we've made some good friends and have sort of become honorary members of the nearby community, the town of Bella Villa. The Cokers are great landlords, sufficiently friendly but not in-your-face. Sam, the county sheriff and Joe, one of his deputies, drop in on occasion. Duane, the proprietor of The Rabbit Hole, the town's primary restaurant, invites us to all of his Welsh Rabbit Parties. And, back in Alexandria, Buddy of the local grocery store, provides us with slightly brown apples to feed the critters. Much of our acceptance by the locals is due to Chuck Hadaman, a townie who makes his living as Chief of Facilities at DoTI. On any given weekend, it would not be unusual to find one or more of those people visiting us or to find us socializing in Bella Villa, sometimes accompanied by Buddy. We love it.

I pulled into the driveway, past the Coker's house, and onto a gravel pad next to the cabin. We unloaded the trunk, inspected our little kitchen garden (which the Cokers thoughtfully keep from ruin) and entered. A bottle of Chianti Reserva, some cheddar, and crackers awaited us. Life was lovely.

Alex got up to peer out the window to see what was going on in the rural world.

He turned back to me, exclaiming, "But, soft! What light through yonder window breaks. It is the Hadaman."

We went out to find a big gray gelding trotting up with Chuck astride. He dismounted when he reached the cabin and tied the brute up at the river birch just beyond reach of our edibles.

Chuck is a big, rugged looking man. A Gary Cooper type. He has a rumbling baritone voice out of which comes a slight stutter. Once you get used to the stutter you don't notice it.

We ushered him into the cabin and furnished him with wine, cheese, and crackers. "Do you have an agenda?" Alex asked. "Or do you just want to hang out?"

"Both," Chuck said. "As you know, every year I f-f-fabricate something for the homecoming float. Been doing it for nigh onto nine years."

We knew that. We also knew that the town had a contest built around it. People would enter ideas for the fabrication, the mayor and town council would judge the entries, and Chuck would then construct, in metal, the winner. Last year it was a fabrication of a football player, arms and legs pumping, chasing a squealing pig.

Chuck continued. "Not knowing what to do with all those fabrications of the p-p-past – they were taking up space in the mayor's basement – the council decided to make a museum of them."

"Wow!"

"Great!"

Chuck held up his hands. "It's n-n-nothing, nothing at all. Just due tribute to my genius. They're going to have a grand opening in a couple of weeks for the hoi polloi. But there's going to be a pre-opening next Saturday. Would you like to come?"

I grinned. "Would we ever!"

That settled and in appreciation, Alex went out and fed Chuck's horse an apple.

We spent the next couple of hours wandering around the farm and cuddling the alpacas. Around eight o'clock, a bit before it got dark, Chuck retrieved his horse, rode off into the sunset and back to his sister's nearby horse farm.

The Cokers had invited us to a pre-shearing breakfast, so we walked up to their house, where we met Daryl Junior and his wife, Sandy. They had come to help with the shearing. They were a pleasant couple. Junior was a computernik and he and Alex retreated into their own world, until breakfast was ready. Claudia managed to put them at opposite ends of the table, the better to be sociable. During the socializing, I discovered that the Juniors had bought a house on the Eastern Shore in order to be near their mutual employer, Oxford College, where young Daryl was an instructor in the math department and Sandy taught entomology in the biology department. They were both newly minted PhDs, a fact that neither Claudia nor Daryl senior had ever mentioned.

Breakfast was what I had always imagined farmers eating: Perfectly fried eggs, sizzling bacon, hot biscuits topped with homemade gravy, never-ending coffee. It was such a typical farm breakfast that I wondered if Claudia was putting us on. I'm still not sure she wasn't.

After breakfast, we made our way to the big barn. It measured about forty-five feet on the short sides, about eighty feet in length. The entrance was on the short side nearest the house. We entered into a sort of ante-room, about eight feet wide, that ran the width of the structure. A scale hung from a rafter. At the back end were stairs to the loft. A half-height wall jutted out from the stairs toward the other end of the short side for about fifteen feet, did a left turn, ran about sixty-five feet and then made another left turn. This half-height wall thus enclosed an area about fifteen by sixty-five feet. The area was divided into four stalls, each of which had a door to an outdoor extension of the stall. The inside corridor ran beside the stalls, the entire length of the building. At the far end, another door led to the outside part of the stalls. A small room, where the animals' medicines were stored and where the critters were brought for their shots, was carved out of the corridor.

When we got to the barn, we found it buzzing with Coker neighbors, friends, and kids – some from as far as two towns away. Everyone was given a chore. The men, including Alex, were to lead the reluctant animals into the far stall, where they were vacuumed. From there, other men would bring them one at a time to the shearing area.

The animals did not like to get sheared. They seemed to regard it as an affront to their self-esteem and they put up a helluva fuss. But sheared they got. The llamas came first. When the animal reached the shearing area, Daryl and another guy who also knew what he was doing, muscled the beast into an open cage and strapped it in. Daryl then used a wide blade to shear the fleece, which dropped off the llama in sheets.

It is notable that llamas and alpacas are related to camels. Like camels, they spit. With the first llama, a clueless woman standing close to the beast's head, got it right in the kisser. Llama spit smells awful. She ran, puffing and stinking, to the medicine room where Claudia, trying not to laugh, sponged her off. Daryl fitted a little bag over the nose of that and all subsequent animals.

When the shorn llama was being led out the back door, Claudia caught Daryl's attention. "The medicine room is a mess. There's water and paper towels all over the floor. The door to the freezer is open – I think the shots are probably ruined. Who's been in there?"

Daryl had no idea. But the next llama was arriving and the discussion ended.

Once an animal was shorn, its fiber was given to a brigade of women and older kids. The fiber was put into bags, each of which was labeled with the name of its former owner, and the part of the anatomy it came from. The bags were then sealed and one of the younger kids would bring it to me. I would weigh it, record the weight, and drop the record into the bag. Another young kid would run it up the stairs and deposit the bag in the loft. The kid reported to me that the Cokers kept a messy loft.

"Almost looks like some people were fooling around up there."

I didn't know how the kid defined "fooling around" and I didn't want to know.

After the llamas, the alpacas came for their shearing. Unlike llamas, alpacas are sheared while lying on their sides, legs splayed and strapped down. There were lots and lots of alpacas. Most of them unhappy. Some of them spitting. A couple of them, though, seemed to enjoy the process.

Snacks – vegetables and dips, potato chips, cookies, yogurt cups – were set up along the wall. These served as lunch.

About five thirty we finally came to the end of the alpacas and adjourned for dinner in the main house. Claudia had laid out a spread. Big pot of chili, another big pot of lamb stew, salad, ice cream, coffee, tea, cooler tubs of beer and white wine. Red wine was lined up on the counter.

The party broke up about eight. The assemblage departed on foot, in cars, and in pickups.

Alex and I stumbled back to the cabin, exhausted. We just

managed to remove our clothes before we fell into bed. Showers and snoggles could wait until morning.

Sunday was one of those wonderful throw-away days. We spent a lot of time in bed, snoozing and snoggling and whatever. We walked down to the paddock and inspected the critters. They looked strange without their fuzzy coats – kind of tailored. Gertrude came trotting up to Alex, who kissed her nose. She nuzzled him. He gave her an apple. She scooted back to the herd.

"That's good," Alex said. "I was afraid she wouldn't like me any more after I led her to the vacuum." I kissed him.

On Monday, we went to see the Bella Villa Memorial Day Parade. It was the essence of small town parade. The Volunteer Fire Department, bells clanging, siren whooping, was followed by Sam and the County Sheriff's Department which, for the day, had deputized Bella Villa's lone policeman so that he could march with the Sheriff's Department. Sam blew us a kiss as they marched by. The sheriffs were followed by the high school band. They were off-key, but who cared? Then came the mayor and the town council, crammed into a little open-roofed bus This was followed by a WW II Jeep in which sat some seventy- and eighty-year-old veterans of the war of the same name. Younger guys from subsequent wars followed on foot. Those guys were followed by the dolled-up town dogs, horses and riders, the Scouts (Girl and Boy), a line of tractors from the neighboring farms, a scruffy motorcycle towing a wheeled contraption carrying a gigantic snake from the alligator wrestling place, and finally by a very big float displaying all of Chuck's fabrications as well as Chuck himself.

After the parade we went to the town green where the mayor tried to give a speech. He was drowned out by the cries of those in the hungry audience who wanted to get to the pig roast.

I found us a picnic table while Alex tried his muscles at the strength-o-meter. This device has a scale at the base and a tower with markings attached. The player is given a long-handled club with which to whack the scale and then, depending on how hard he is able to whack it, a bulb lights up at the appropriate place on the tower. The harder the whack the higher the lit-up bulb. If the guy hits the scale hard enough, the bulb at the very top lights up, accompanied by whizzes and bangs. Alex was standing there, legs braced, club raised when I looked down.

A very large snake, a python or a Boa constrictor or some such thing, was slithering toward me. A huge, bearded man was helping it along. I did what any fair maiden would do in the circumstances. I screamed.

The huge man laughed. Alex turned, saw what was happening and shouted at the man, "Get that snake out of here!"

The man laughed harder. "Or you'll do what, little fella?"

"This," said Alex. "And brought the club down on the snake's head.

"Goddamn, you killed my snake you sonuvabitch!" He took a step toward Alex, fists clenched. By that time, however, a crowd was between Alex and the giant. The crowd included Sheriff Sam who, by virtue of his office, had a gun. Which was pointed at the giant, who stopped in his tracks.

"Would you care to explain yourself?" Sam said mildly.

"Now," said the man, "there's no need to take offense. I was just funnin' the lady.   There was no call to kill my pet Boa."

"That's part of the explanation," Sam said.   "And what made you decide to 'fun' this particular lady?"

"Well now, I dunno that I want to tell you that."

"That's your privilege," said Sam. He turned to Joe, who had walked up beside him.

"Cuff him."

"You arrestin' me?" The man was outraged.

"Yep," said Sam.

Joe cuffed the guy.

"What the hell for?"

"For starters," Sam explained, "reckless endangerment, bringing a wild animal into a public place, and I don't know what else the hell for. I'll think of something."

"But I gotta get back to my business.   This is a big payday for us."

Sam smiled.   "What made you decide to 'fun' this particular lady," he repeated.

The giant gave up.   "I found an envelope in my mailbox.   It had a hunnert dollar bill in it and a paper with a description of the lady – not too many ladies with that reddy-brown color hair.   Note said they wanted to play a joke on her and I should scare her with a snake.   It was just a joke."

"You got the note?"

"Yeah, but I spent the hunnert."

"Okay," said Sam.   "You got the note with you?"

The guy shook his head.   "It's at the business."

"First, pick up that reptile and put it in the cage. Then let's go get that note."

"Can't pick up no snake with cuffs on."

Joe removed the cuffs.   Sam did not lower the gun. The dead snake was returned to the cage.   The guy was re-cuffed and the three men got into Sam's cruiser and departed. One of the other deputies revved up the giant's motorcycle, attached the cage, and followed after.

No doubt about it.   Bella Villa knows how to throw a pig roast.

Deputy Joe stopped by our cabin after the roast.   He looked serious. We sat him down and fed him a beer.   "What's going on, Joe?"

"A retarded kid's gone missing from home in Bella Villa.   He's wandered off before, so no one was much worried.   He always comes back.   We were sure he'd turn up for the parade and the roast.   But there's no sign of him.

"We've pretty much looked all over the town and the little woods just outside of town.   Tomorrow we're going to search farther. We've got some volunteers rounded up and we'll organize a manhunt."

"How can we help?" Alex asked.

Joe shook his head.   "We've got plenty of volunteers.   But if you see a kid wandering around while you're on the way to work, would you call the station?   I don't know how far he could've got in two days – he's on foot. He's about eleven years old, five feet tall. He was wearing jeans and a red jacket. Real friendly. His name is Petey."

CHAPTER 7

May 26, 1992

We said good-bye to the critters, got into the Mustang, and proceeded up the hill toward LIT. These long rural weekends are fun, if you exclude the creepy crawlers.

I pulled into the LIT parking lot. We had settled in for a good-by snoggle when there was a rapping on Alex's window. We looked out at Chrissie and her dad.

Alex lowered the window. "Are we interrupting something?" Chrissie asked.

"No, no, of course not," Alex said.

She's a great kid, but I may smack her one.

"I just wanted to tell Dr. Goode that this is my first day as an intern."

"That's great, Chrissie," I said. "If you have time, stop by around lunchtime and let me know how things are going."

Jim was standing behind his offspring trying, but failing, to look innocent.

We got out of the car. Alex and Chrissie walked toward the Centers. Jim and I walked toward the Admin wing. "I'm sorry," Jim said, looking not at all contrite, "but I couldn't resist."

"Just wait'll your performance review comes up, buster."

He peeled off toward his office and I stopped at mine. There were two voice messages for me. One from Julia. "I'm sorry, Bea. I had no idea she could be such an ass. Even if she thought it, she should have had the sense not to say it. I don't really think she's suited for a policy position." Julia Han, master of understatement.

The other message was from Marcy, apologizing. "I was out of line. I'm just so upset about Mapledent..."

I returned Julia's call. We agreed that it was best we found out now in case we were ever called upon to recommend Marcy for anything that required diplomacy.

The gods were on my side; Marcy was out when I called her. I left a message saying that I fully understood. I didn't specify just what I understood.

I picked up three copies of Pie's briefing paper and brought them to his office. We called Don to join us. While we were waiting for Don, Pie informed me that Bessie was flying in from Ecuador that night. Pie would pick her up at the airport.

Bessie, Pie's wife, is an eminent archeologist, frequently asked to supervise digs in remote places. She is kind of a free-lance archeologist. She is much in demand, I suspect, not just for her expertise (which is considerable) but for her equable, unflappable disposition. She has some kind of arrangement with the Smithsonian, which provides her with an office and lab in exchange for occasional consulting. When Bessie wasn't off somewhere being eminent, she and Pie played house.

"Do you and Alex want to get together with us this weekend?" Pie asked.

I told him about Chuck's museum pre-opening. "Why don't we get together there?"

"Will that be okay with Chuck?"

"Of course. Let's find out if it's okay with Aunt Bessie. If it is, we can make the arrangements tomorrow morning."

At that point, Don walked in and the two men looked over the data.

"I don't have a good answer for the Louisianans," Pie said. "That's not a decision I can make."

"They won't be looking for a decision," Don remarked, "they'll be trying to get you on their side when decision time comes."

"Yeah. I don't like to stonewall, but I don't know what else I can do. I'm not in the loop on this one."

I thought. "Why don't you just tell them that you're not in the loop and, in any event, the Administration might change shortly. You understand what the problem is, you're sympathetic, but there's nothing you can do and you don't have anyone's ear on this issue."

Don looked at me. "And you think they'll be satisfied with that?"

"No. But they won't be satisfied with anything else, either."

Pie said, "At least Bea's suggestion has the virtue of being true."

Don nodded. "Yeah. But that virtue is going to be its own reward."

We batted the problem around for a while. Pie finally said, "I'll dazzle them with my knowledge of the statistics and go with the virtuous truth. I think that will at least keep our budget out of trouble."

And with that, the discussion ended.

Pie then asked me, "How are you going to handle Mapledent?"

"I'm going to pretend it never happened. I'm just going to let him think that no one took the complaint seriously enough to talk to me about it."

Don snickered. "That'll drive the slime bag nuts."

"Yep. It will indeed."

Chrissie didn't appear that morning. Good. They were keeping her busy.

I coaxed the clunker out of the lot and picked up Julia and Billy.

"Do both of you have waders?" Julia asked.   We both did.

"Why do you ask?"

"I thought it might be fun to get a little closer to the marsh where we can see some of the amphibians up close and personal. There's one little frog that's no bigger than my thumbnail.   And the American bullfrogs are two-toned.   Green spots on brown or green head and brown body.   The first time I saw one of those, it was sitting with its rump in mud and its head in greenery.   I thought it was like a chameleon, changing color.   But then I found out that its location was just coincidence. The guy always had a green head and brown body."

"I'd like to see the sights.   I'll throw the waders in the car trunk when I get home," I said.

Julia then handed me the picture of Drumm and Farrington, beautifully framed.   "Lovely!   I shall hang it in a place of honor in my office."

Dexter Hamilton greeted us when we arrived at Cabot House.   He smiled at me.   "Elaine Ickes asked me to give you her warm regards."

"Thank you.   If you talk with her in the near future, please return the sentiment."

"I'll certainly do that."

"Who's Elaine Ickes?" Billy asked.

"A mutual friend.   She works at IBM."

The DRA contingent was awaiting us in the conference room.   I opened the meeting and asked if anyone had any tweaking for the mission statement.   Howie Farrington opened his mouth and Billy, who was sitting next to him, silenced him with a look. Howie closed his mouth.

"Well then, will someone move that we accept it."

"So move," said Julia.

"Second," said Howie.

Billy pretended to write that down. He then read the minutes of the last meeting, including Mapledent's objection to inviting HBCUs to the party. Mapledent asked to have that expunged. "I've thought better of that," he explained.

"Well," Billy said, "we can't rewrite history but I can put your retraction in *these* minutes."

Mapledent compressed his lips.

"Okay," I said, "let us continue. Doug could you retire to your sitting room and start on the Goals and Objectives? Come back about four thirty and we'll review them."

"May I ask a question?" he said.

"Of course."

"I'm not trying to be a trouble maker..."

No, of course not.

"...but why is Fisheries represented on the Committee? It is not part of DRA."

"No, I responded, "but it *is* part of DoTI and is a significant element in both trade and industry. Global warming will have a huge effect on fish. When the sea level rises, the ocean temperature rises, the fish move to higher latitudes, the acidity of the water increases, the CO_2 increases – all sorts of things happen."

Billy nodded agreement.

"It seems," said G. Douglas, "that you have anticipated the work of the contractors."

"Not at all," said Billy. "There is no question but that all of that will happen. The question is what effect will it have? I'm keeping NOAA informed of what we're doing. If Bea gets out of line, someone there who knows something will correct her."

Mapledent half rose. "Are you implying that I don't know something?"

"You two can duke that out later." *Whoops. Unfortunate phrasing.* "Meanwhile, Doug, please start working on the Goals and Objectives."

Mapledent stalked off.

"All right, let's begin discussing the questions that the contractors should address. Treat the first part of the discussion as a brainstorming session. Just throw out questions, no critical judgments at this stage. We'll examine each question critically when we run out of ideas."

"Dr. Goode," Emmaline said, "I think that this whole global warming thing is God's Will and we shouldn't interfere."

I had been waiting for that one. "We all agree that this is God's Will, Emmaline. But God's Will has to be interpreted, the same way that Christians and Jews both interpret the bible. The purpose of this study is to contribute to the interpretation."

"But," said Emmaline, and stopped.

"But what?" Howie asked.

Emmaline looked confused. "Nothing," she said.

Julia started the brainstorming. "What areas will be helped and what areas will be harmed by global warming?"

Billy: What species will be lost?

Howie: Can we expect an acceleration in diseases?

Billy: Can the depletion of the ozone layer be reversed?

At which point the door opened and Dexter Hamilton entered. "I'm sorry to interrupt, but a crisis has developed. A retarded eleven-year-old boy has been missing from his home in Bella Villa since last weekend. They've been looking for him since then, but now they've broadened the search area and a manhunt will reach Cabot House shortly. I'm afraid you're going to be disrupted."

I asked Hamilton how we could help. He told us that volunteers had spread through the countryside. The sheriff and his deputies would cover the marsh – they were properly equipped to deal with the water. The Cabot House staff would search the house and the immediate grounds. If it was okay with me, it would be a help if the Committee people could search the area bordering the trail around the lake and marsh, the flat area where the ferns might conceivably hide a boy, and the slope up through the trees. He departed to direct his staff.

Howie went to get Mapledent and we all trooped through the grounds to the wetland. Sam was there directing the marsh contingent. He welcomed the reinforcements.

Mapledent volunteered to do the slope, with Emmaline's assistance. The rest of us were deployed to the area bordering the trail, including the part covered by ferns. Sam gave us policeman's whistles to be used if we found anything.

Howie and I took the path running from the left of the boardwalk; Julia and Billy went right. It was painstaking work. We covered every inch of the ground surrounding the entire lake and the marsh (deputies were wading and thrashing there), and the dry area below the slope, where we linked up with Julia and Billy. Nothing. Mapledent and Emmaline descended from the slope. More nothing. We were looking helplessly at one another when the sound of a whistle came from the marsh. We ran toward the sound.

The search party had found bones, picked clean, and seemingly not scattered too far. Sam was directing that they be handled carefully and bagged. Mapledent asked if it was the boy.

"I don't know, sir. I think the size of the femur and the pelvis would be consistent with the boy's stature and gender, but I'm not qualified to do forensic analysis. We'll send what we find to the State lab."

Mapledent grunted. "Well, I don't suppose there would be two male skeletons of that size hanging around."

"No, sir. I expect you're right. But I will check, just to be sure." Mapledent shrugged and walked off.

Joe appeared. "Sam, we found the skull. It's intact."

"Teeth?"

"Yes," Joe answered.

"That'll make it easier. There must be dental records to compare. But keep searching, we should get all of the bones we can find. The parents will want as much of their boy as we can salvage."

Joe motioned Sam to follow him. After a short conference, Sam returned to the group, thanked us for the help, and suggested that we leave. We started off when Sam called me back. I asked Billy and Julia to wait for me in the conference room.

"What's up, Sam?"

"You guys were of so much help the last time I got in over my head, do you think we can use you as consultants on this one? As you may have noticed, we're just a small county force that handles traffic accidents and domestics real well."

"I don't know what help we can be, but we'll do whatever we can. What's the problem?"

Sam sighed. "What was bothering me as soon as we found the

bones was that there was no sign of clothing or anything else that might serve as identification. Do you know if whatever ate the flesh might also have eaten the clothing and shoes?"

"I don't know. But Billy Norman might – he's the aquatic expert. He and my other team member are waiting for me in the conference room."

Sam beckoned to one of his deputies and sent him to retrieve Billy and Julia.

He turned back to me and said, "There's no question but that this was murder. The skull Joe found had been hit by some heavy instrument. The blow was in the back, not on the top, of the head. Nothing accidentally fell on it. Someone had it in for the kid."

I thought about that. "If those bones do, in fact, belong to the kid. This may be the work of some pervert, but other than that, I can't think of any reason why someone would kill a retarded boy."

Sam nodded. "And it would be a strange way for a pervert to kill the kid, unless the kid were running away and the pervert caught up with him. But except for that, you'd think the killer would do something like strangle him. He isn't a husky kid."

"Do you know him?"

"Yeah. The missing boy is Petey Petrofsky. His folks run the hardware store in Bella Villa. Nice people. I sure don't want to tell them that Petey is dead."

The deputy returned with Billy, Julia and Howie in tow.

Howie's presence was unexpected. "I thought you went back with Doug and Emmaline."

"I couldn't face another lesson in Creationism from that silly girl. Doug eggs her on – he thinks it's funny. I was begging Julia or Billy to drop me at a Metro stop on their way home when the deputy came to get them, so I tagged along."

"Alex and I pass right by New Carrollton. We can drop you there."

Julia said, "I go within a half mile of Howie's house. If he rides with us to DoTI, it's no problem for me to chauffeur him the rest of the way."

"Done."

I explained to them about the missing clothes. "Billy, would something in the marsh have eaten or otherwise disposed of all the clothes and the shoes?"

"Not impossible but not likely. Those bones were picked clean by a combination of snapping turtles and crayfish, but mostly by snails. Possible that some critters – raccoons maybe – might have hauled them off, but you'd expect that something would have been left behind."

He turned to Sam. "Did you find any scraps of cloth or leather?"

"Nothing."

"Then it's unlikely, given that the body has been in the marsh for less than a week. I'm surprised that the carrion birds weren't hovering."

Sam remarked, "This has been a full week for road kill. The vultures had better restaurants to dine at.

"Well, we'll find out if it's Petey as soon as we get the dental records – today or tomorrow, probably. But if it isn't Petey – who in the world is it? The State will take a long time to do the forensics. This has been a bad year not just for car accidents, but at least four little planes have dropped out of the sky in the last couple of months and no one knows who the passengers were. Our skeleton is going to have to get in line."

"Maybe not," I said. "Bessie will be back in the country tonight.

She's used to dealing with much older bones, but she might be willing to take a crack at this batch."

Sam, who knew and adored Bessie, beamed. "That would be great. As soon as I find out if it's Petey, I'll call you. If it's not him, would you ask Bessie?"

"Absolutely."

Julia entered the conversation. "Are you treating this as a crime scene? We were planning to explore the marsh sometime soon. Can we still do that?"

Sam nodded. "No point in putting the marsh off-limits. There won't be any footprints in a marsh and we've already picked up everything there is to pick up – which, except for the bones, is zilch."

I asked Sam, "Can we take off now?"

He nodded.

"When we explore the marsh, if we should find something that your guys missed, we'll save it for you."

"Thank you, ma'am. I'll be in touch as soon as I know something." Sam gave me a peck on the cheek and went off to join his deputies.

On the return trip to DoTI, we decided to start Thursday's meeting at ten in the morning, to make up for today's shortened session. Howie said he'd inform Doug and Emmaline. I would ask Cabot House to give us a light lunch and then reconvene the meeting at two o'clock. Between lunch and two o'clock, we would do our marsh tour – DRA could join us or else catch up on whatever phone calls had accumulated in their offices. Julia reminded us to bring our waders. She'd bring the camera. Howie regretted that he couldn't come wading, but he needed the time to prepare for an early meeting the following morning. Since Howie couldn't come, we decided to make it a strictly DoTI tour.

Alex looked immensely pleased with himself when we met at the Mustang. He gave me an exuberant kiss as we entered out chariot. "What's the good news?" I asked him.

He grinned. "Fred just reported giant strides in voice recognition. We're on our way!"

"Fred the Cookie Monster?"

"The very same."

For most of the way home, Alex described equations and algorithms and goodness knows whatall. I didn't understand a bit of it, but nodded and exclaimed in what seemed to be the right places. The man deserved an interested ear when reporting a triumph. As we reached our neighborhood he wound up with, "And we'll be sure to get one of the big Awards."

A thought struck me. "Do you think Fred could come to the Award ceremony as the Cookie Monster?"

Alex scowled. "There are some things, my dear, that we just don't joke about."

I didn't get a chance to tell him about the skeleton until we were finishing the last of the Moroccan lentil soup.

CHAPTER 8

May 27, 1992

I popped into Pie's office to give him a quick update.

Bessie was seated on the sofa when I arrived. I sat down next to her and we embraced. She was an attractive, plump, little woman, browned from her days on the dig. "Was Ecuador fruitful?" I asked.

"Yes and no. We're talking about the Inca empire now. The last Inca emperor, Atahualpa, is entombed somewhere in the Andes. He was captured and killed by the Spaniards in Peru. There is some reason to believe that his followers brought the body to Ecuador and entombed him there. The Ecuadorian archeologists think they have located the general area where that happened.

"We examined much of the ground and found some very suggestive artifacts, but nothing definitive. The team will continue to poke around and if anything looks really promising, I'll go back and help with the dig."

As usual, after talking with Bessie, I regretted not being an archeologist.

I turned to Pie. "How did it go with the Louisianans?"

"As well as could be expected. I followed your advice and punted. They were disappointed but understanding. They left hoping for better things with a new Administration.

"How was your day?"

"Well," I started and went on to describe the manhunt and the skeleton. "We'll know soon enough if it's the Petrofsky kid, but I have my doubts."

"What's sticking in your craw?" Pie asked.

"Nothing for certain. The lack of clothing is troubling. Why would Petey's killer try to hide the kid's identity? Anyone finding the body would assume it was Petey. As they have. Sam is just being careful. Also, the absence of hovering vultures doesn't ring true. Sure, there's been a lot of road kill, but that doesn't mean the birds would pass this up. At least a few of them might have noticed that there wasn't much competition for the carrion.

"Hovering vultures would have been noticed if they had been there shortly after Petey disappeared and the site would have been investigated right away. If the body isn't Petey, but someone who had been there for a longer time, though, the birds would have been dismissed as just being after some critter that drowned in the marsh."

Bessie eyed me. "For a sedentary bureaucrat," she said, "you certainly lead an exciting life. So they don't know if the bones belong to the boy?"

"No. But they've got a skull full of teeth and Petey's dentist is probably available, so they should know shortly. If it turns out to be someone else, would you be willing to look at the bones and tell Sam what you find?"

"For Sam? Sure. What condition are the bones in?"

"Picked clean by wetland creatures," I answered. "Sam had the bones carefully bagged."

"Good. Too bad we don't know yet if the teeth match the boy's. If they don't, I could have looked at the bones today. I'm on my way in to the Smithsonian. They know I'm coming, so my lab should be free."

Pie said, "Let's call Sam and find out when he'll have the

information." He put the phone on speaker.

Sam picked up on the first ring. "I was just about to call Bea. It's not Petey."

Bessie cut in. "This is Bessie. I'm on my way to my lab in Washington. If you can get me the bones now, I'll have a look."

"Hey, Bessie, I can't tell you how good it is to hear your voice. I'll have the bones to you ASAP." We heard Sam call for a deputy.

I entered the conversation. "When the deputy gets here, have him park in the nearest lot. When he gets out of the car, he should turn left to the Admin wing and then ask anyone he sees to point him to Pie's office."

"That'll be done," Sam said.

"Don't hang up," I said. "Did you find out anything about the woman who was killed?"

"She wasn't raped," Sam answered. "There was nothing anywhere around to give us a clue. She apparently was on her way to school, but there wasn't anything in the car. No school files. No handbag. Nothing except a leaf. Looks like it might have been a straightforward robbery. We may never know."

Sam disconnected.

"What was that all about?" Pie asked.

I explained. As is often the case when something bad happens to someone you don't know, we talked about it for a minute or two and then went back to something more immediate.

While we waited for the bones to arrive, we discussed the upcoming event at Hadaman's museum. "I'd like to bring Jim and Chrissie, if they can make it and if it's okay with Chuck."

"That would be good," Pie said. "They've been having a rough time of it. They deserve some fun."

We decided that we would all meet on Saturday at Pie's house and would go together in his car, which would easily hold all six of us. If Don and Connie wanted to come, we'd go in two cars.

"Bring waders. If we detour to Cabot House, I can show you all the Wonders of the Wetland."

A non sequitur occurred to me. "Bessie," I said, "in your long and illustrious career, were you discriminated against because you were a woman?"

Bessie looked at me as if she thought I had lost my mind. "Of course. And Pie was discriminated against because he's a Jewish Chinaman. And I'm sure that splendid horticulturalist of Molly's was discriminated against because he's Black. And if you tell me you were never discriminated against I won't believe you."

I thought about it for a minute. "Yeah, I guess you're right. It never bothered me much, though. I just went around it."

"Difference in technique," Bessie said. "I didn't go around it. I bulled through it. Why did you ask?"

I told her about Marcy.

"Hmph," she hmphed. "So her method of coping is to *kvetch* and blame the silly kid? Good luck to her."

Bessie thought for a bit and said, "You know, Pie and I are in our fifties. I'll bet within our lifetime it will not be unusual for minorities to be heads of state – Margaret Thatcher, Sirimavo Bandaranaike, Indira Ghandi – have already broken the ground in that department – and heads of Fortune 500 companies that do something besides sell cosmetics. There will be some momentarily successful resisters, like that petty satrap Mapledent, but we minorities will prove that we can be just as capable, as trustworthy, as brilliant, as stupid, as warlike, as corrupt, as obdurate as

99

the men."

I laughed. "Of course. We're all people."

I scooted back to my office and called Chuck. He was fine with all of us attending the pre-opening. He told me that the museum was located right next to the courthouse, in the unused building that once housed the town's information center. The information center had been moved to a new building, visible from the highway.

Then I called Jim, who called Chrissie, who called me. She confirmed that they would join us.

"Do you have waders?" I asked.

"Sort of," Chrissie answered. "There's a pair that belonged to my Mom. They almost fit me." On that, we hung up.

I was about to visit Ben for a look at the data on forest exports when my phone once more sprang into action. It was Howie.

"Hey, Bea. Do they know if it's the kid?"

"It's not. Dental records don't match the teeth in the skull. The bones will be examined later today."

"Good," Howie said. "I think I know who they belong to."

"Really? Who?"

"I'm at a small meeting here at DRA and a Georgetown U. botanist, Craig Thibodeau, was supposed to give an informal talk at nine. He's been on a walking tour of the Blue Ridge. He was expected to be back last night. This morning, he was going to tell us if he found anything new and unusual and show us some slides. He hasn't shown up or called. He's a real little guy – could be mistaken for an eleven-year-old boy. If it's not the kid from Bella Villa, Craig is a good candidate."

"Thanks! That's great information. It will save Sam a ton of time if it proves out. Have you told Mapledent?"

"Damn. I just plumb forgot." Howie laughed and hung up.

I left my office and was headed toward Ben's room when the outside door opened and Sam's deputy arrived carrying a large case, presumably filled with bags of bones.

"Hello, Dr. Goode. I'm Walt. I'm supposed to give this to Dr. Lee. Do you know where his office is?

"I do. Follow me and I will take you to my Lee-der."

"Is that supposed to be funny?"

"Yes, it is."

Having received permission, Walt laughed.

We marched down the hall and Walt deposited his burden on Lenore's desk. We summoned Bessie, who signed for the package, and Walt left. Bessie brought the case into Pie's office.

"What's in there?" Lenore asked.

I said, "Bones."

"Yeah, sure." Lenore said.

Pie and Bessie emerged from the office, Pie carrying the bones. "I'm carrying this to the car."

Lenore asked him, "What's in the case?"

"Bones," said Pie.

Lenore looked at me, shaking her head. "Don't you people ever stop kidding around?"

I finally remembered that I had the photo of Drumm and Farrington sitting next to my computer. I stopped in the supply room, found a hook-and-nail assembly and strode purposefully to my office. I looked around for something with which to bang the nail into the wall. The stapler would do. I had just climbed onto a chair when Ben entered.

He had finally despaired of my ever arriving at his place, so he came to me instead, his statistical offerings in hand. He was wearing his Daffy Duck tie. He watched critically as I positioned the nail and clobbered it into the wall.

"Is this the picture you're hanging?" He held up Julia's masterpiece.

"That's it."

Ben examined the photo. "This man," he said as he handed it to me, "is being falsely accused."

I knew better but I asked anyway. "What makes you say that?"

"Clearly, he's been framed."

He left the papers on the computer table and departed.

I completed my interior decorating, sat down at my desk and immersed myself in import/export numbers.

After lunch, no sooner had I resumed my immersion, than the phone rang. It was Claudia Coker.

"Bea, I'm sorry to bother you at work, but Sam thought you should know this. He's on his way to a bad accident so he asked me to call and tell you about it."

"Tell me about what?"

"They found Petey. He's okay."

"Thank goodness! Where was he?"

"It wasn't easy to get a straight story from him, but here's what they've been able to piece together.

"Friday was a beautiful night and Petey woke up, looked out the window at the stars, and decided to go out for a better look at them. He got dressed, star-gazed for a while, and then went off into the woods somewhere between Bella Villa and our farm. After a while, he got drowsy so he lay down under the trees and went to sleep.

"It was still dark when he finished napping, but he got up despite the dark and kept walking until he got to the road. He was heading our way when some guy in a pickup stopped and asked him if he wanted a lift."

"Would Petey get into a truck with a stranger?"

"He's not supposed to go anywhere with a stranger. But Petey loves trucks so he said yes. It was getting light when the truck got to our place. Petey recognized the driveway and asked to be let out. The guy evidently thought Petey lived here and dropped him off. Anyway, that's how Petey managed to get so far from home. He wasn't walking.

"So when the guy dropped him off, Petey strolled past our house, opened the door to the barn and went in. He washed up and went to the bathroom in the room where we store the medicine. He left the room in a mess, the little bugger. Then he went up to the loft, rearranged things to his liking, and had himself another nap.

"By that time Junior and Sandy had arrived, parked their pickup, and came into the house to wait for breakfast.

"Petey noticed the truck, but he had a few other things he wanted to do before he explored this new truck. He looked at the alpacas for a while, looked around that little patch of wetland on the property, went back into the woods and snacked on wild berries for breakfast. We can thank our lucky stars that he didn't eat anything poisonous! He didn't even get himself a case of poison ivy.

"Our guess is that he played around in the woods almost all day and about the time we served dinner, he went back into the barn, stuffed himself with leftover snacks, and went to the bathroom again. It was something like that.   The room was messed up again just after I'd cleaned it.

"He probably remembered Junior's truck after that. But whenever he remembered, he climbed into the back of the pickup and went to sleep."

"And all that time, no one saw him?" I asked.

"Except for the guy who gave him a lift, not a soul.   Don't know why that guy hasn't come forward, but he hasn't.   The alarm's been sounded on television, the radio, the newspapers, and on posters."

"The guy was in a truck.   He may have been traveling too far to have heard anything."

"Makes sense.   Anyhow, while Petey was sleeping in the back, Junior and Sandy drove the truck to Oxford on the Eastern shore."

"Good heavens!"

"Wait, there's more," Claudia said. "Petey had a high old time in Oxford.   That's not a big city, bigger than Bella Villa, but not so big that people lock their doors.   Even some shopkeepers are careless about it.   And Oxford is far enough away so that nobody paid any attention to the news that a kid was missing from Bella Villa.

"Petey wandered around town for days. He said he looked at lots of things.   He even went into a book store and a sweet gray-haired lady gave him some good candy. He thinks Oxford is a very nice place.

"At night he said he sometimes walked into people's houses while they were asleep and helped himself to stuff in their refrigerators, or he got into closed but not locked grocery stores or delis, had a meal, used their facilities, and filled his pockets with things to eat the next day.   When it got late enough and he got sleepy enough, he went down to the University boathouse and went to sleep in a beached boat.

"Finally, about nine this morning he decided that he'd seen enough

of Oxford and found a hardware store that looked a little like the
Petrofsky's. He walked in and informed the proprietor that he was ready
to go home now. He gave the proprietor the card with his name and
phone number that's always pinned to his jacket.

"The proprietor called the Talbott County sheriff and he called
Sam. One of Sam's patrol cars drove out to Oxford and picked Petey up.
The Petrofskys didn't know whether to kiss him or kill him."

I laughed. "Or both."

"Or both," Claudia agreed.

I called Don and together we went to Pie's office, where I regaled
them with the Perambulations of Petey Petrofsky.

"*Gevalt!*" said Pie.

"Good God!" said Don.

"Amen," said I.

I went back to my numbers and bored myself blue until it was time
to go home.

Alex and I had serious decisions to make on the way to Alexandria.
We had finished the Moroccan lentil soup so the first decision was
whether we should eat out or stop at the deli and pick up something to eat
at home. Eating out is more satisfactory, but getting deli would give me
time to cook something for the morrow's dinner. Deli won.

Next decision concerned the menu. Sausage and black bean soup?
Grecian beef stew? They took about the same amount of time to make.
This was a decision not to be taken lightly. We finally came down on the
side of beef stew, since we had just finished a soup.

We picked up our meal for the evening, stopped at the butcher
shop for stew meat, and at the grocery store for the rest of the ingredients.

Buddy, the grocer, asked if we could use some apples for the alpacas. We could.

Buddy looked at the assemblage of stuff that we had placed on the counter. "What are you making?"

"Grecian beef stew. Would you like to join us for dinner tomorrow?"

Buddy grinned. "Thought you'd never ask. What time?'

"Right around now," Alex said. "Since it's nearly closing time, we'll stop and pick you up and you can close for the day."

"That's swell. I'll bring some salad and the wine."

Leaving, Alex and I turned back as one. "But not screwtop!"

CHAPTER 9

May 28 and May 29, 1992

As we hurried through breakfast, I asked Alex "Who was that idiot who called a morning meeting at Cabot House?"

Alex scowled at me. "It was your evil twin."

We wolfed the rest of the pancakes, rinsed off, dumped the dishes in the sink, and hurried to the car. I then ran back to the house to get our waders. Threw them in the trunk, took my assigned seat behind the wheel, and got the Mustang on the road.

Alex immediately fell asleep. I longed to join him in that activity.

To save time, I picked Julia and Billy up on the way to LIT. No snoggles on this day, though I did find the time to give my beamish boy a quick farewell kiss. But still, the day didn't seem right without a snoggle.

Julia, Billy, and I got into the clunker and made our sedate way to Cabot House. The DRA contingent had not yet arrived. The staff brought us coffee, tea, and pastries while we waited for them. When they finally did get there, Emmaline was not with them.

Mapledent apologized. "We waited quite a while for Emmaline and she never appeared. Then just before we left, I flipped through my phone messages and I found one from her saying that she'd meet us here. But I don't see her."

"Is her car here?" Billy asked.

"I don't know what she drives, but there is an extra car in the front lot – an old Plymouth."

I got up. "I'll ask Mr. Hamilton if he's seen her."

Before I made it to the door, Hamilton came in. He told us that Emmaline had called the previous day and asked if it would be all right if she got here early and did some exploring. She asked him to tell the Committee to start without her if she was a little late.

That mystery solved, I called the meeting to order and Billy took out his Minutes pad. Mapledent departed for his rendezvous with Goals and Objectives.

The four remaining members continued the brainstorming session that began at the last meeting. By noon, we had both compiled a list of about twenty-five questions to be subjected to critical examination and had forgotten completely about Emmaline.

At noon, the Cabot House staff, assisted by G. Douglas, wheeled in trays of lunch. The man had actually been cooperative. He had helped plan the menu, loaded the trays, and assisted in the distribution of the goodies, which consisted of three kinds of tea sandwiches (egg salad, shrimp, and mushroom), marinated lamb skewers, crab dip, crudites, fruit plate.... The DRA Secretary must really have read him the riot act.

He smiled at me. "No hard feelings, big momma. I was flat out wrong. It's hard for an old Southern boy like me to get used to the new order. I'm kind of a slow learner, but eventually it sinks in."

I held out my hand and we shook. We sat down, basking in the warm glow of good feeling, and tucked in.

It was while we were wondering how we were going to eat everything, that we remembered Emmaline.

Julia noted that she, Billy, and I were going to tour the wetland, and we would send Emmaline back to the House when we came across her. She pointed out that wetlands were fascinating places to explore and the young woman probably just lost track of time. Mapledent was unforgiving. "She was supposed to be here for business. No excuses."

We stuffed ourselves as full as we could be stuffed and went to get our waders, telling Howie and Mapledent that the meeting would resume at two. G. Douglas reminded us that we had a lot to get through in the afternoon – we shouldn't dawdle too long.

From the boardwalk, we went right, skirting the lake, where we thought we saw a river otter, and then descending to the edge of the marsh with Julia pointing out the sights. We ascended once more, this time to the flat area where we had observed Drumm and Howie having their disagreement. That area, which was covered with lady and Christmas ferns, served as a transition from the marsh to the wooded area above.

We stopped while Julia took pictures. It was shortly after we arrived at the other side of the marsh that we heard the cries.

"Help!! Get them off me! Get them off me! Help!!"

We ran deeper into the marsh, toward the voice. Emmaline was there, sitting in the water, flicking at places on her body. The woman was covered with leeches. Billy picked her up and started to remove the nauseating worms. I stopped him. "That will take longer than bringing her up to Cabot House and summoning an ambulance".

Julia said, "When you get there, you can pour salt on them. That'll get them off."

Billy shook his head. "It's not too likely, but sometimes if you pour salt, the leeches will vomit the contents of their stomachs into the wounds and cause infection."

I turned tu Julia. "Could you run ahead to Cabot House and call an ambulance?"

I looked at Emmaline in Billy's arms. One of her legs was dangling strangely below the hem of her flowered skirt.

"Julia, tell the dispatcher about the leeches and that there may be a broken leg."

Julia took off, running amazingly quickly in her waders. Billy, Emmaline, and I moved much more slowly.

"Emmaline," I asked, "can you tell us what happened?"

Emmaline was sobbing. "Please get them off me now."

"The emergency technicians will have the instruments to get rid of them without causing infection," I said. A hopeful guess on my part.

Between sobs, Emmaline told us that she had tripped on a tree root among the ferns and had hurt her leg when she fell. She couldn't stand up. She was calling for help when she heard someone running toward her from behind. She thought it was someone coming to help. That's all she remembered.

"Then I woke up in the marsh with those awful things all over me and my leg and my head hurting really bad."

By that time we were approaching Cabot House. Dexter Hamilton and members of the staff, carrying a stretcher, were running toward us. Hamilton told Billy to put Emmaline on the stretcher and directed his staff to get her into a large, first-floor bathroom and to keep her as comfortable as possible until the ambulance arrived. "It will be here any minute," he said.

They carted Emmaline off. He then inspected Billy. "I'll bring you to a bathroom with a shower stall. Take your clothes off and wash yourself down good. Better wash your hair, too; there will be shampoo there. A terry cloth robe will also be in the bathroom. Use it while the staff washes and dries your clothes. I'll call the House nurse. He'll look you over to make sure that you don't have any leeches clinging to you."

He walked off with Billy. Julia had joined us, along with

Mapledent and Howie.   I repeated Emmaline's narrative.

"What a terrible thing to happen to the girl," Howie said.

"Did she see who hit her on the head?" Mapledent asked.

"No.   Whoever it was came up from behind."

"I'm not a superstitious woman," Julia remarked, "but I think this place is jinxed."

A staff member wheeled up a serving dolly.   "Would you like coffee and tea in the conference room?   Dr. Norman can join you there as soon as the nurse checks him over."

We repaired to the conference room.   Within minutes, we heard the ambulance signal its arrival.   I met the emergency medical technicians in the hall and followed them to Emmaline's room.   I told her that things would be okay, that we'd find out who did this to her, and that I'd visit her in the hospital.   I returned to the conference room.

Picking up the conversation, I said, "I don't know about a jinx, but something insalubrious is going on here.   Until we find out what it is, we'll have our meetings at LIT, starting next Tuesday."

"You are intending to meet at LIT?" Mapledent asked.

"Yes," I said.   "Julia is just south of us; you and Howie are just north.   Neither place is convenient for Billy."

"I object," Mapledent said.   "I have been making a monumental effort to be cooperative, but it is unreasonable to ask me to drive all that way."

"It isn't 'all that way,'" Julia responded.   "You are closer to LIT than you are to Cabot House."

"This discussion," Mapledent said, "is between Dr. Goode and myself.   I would appreciate it if you would allow us to resume."

"Doug," I said, "you can run your DRA meetings anyway you like.

But at LIT, we treat our colleagues with respect. Julia is a member of this team."

"I have had enough," Mapledent said. "Please accept my resignation from the Committee."

"You will have to offer the resignation to whomever appointed you. I do not have the authority to deal with it. But I will certainly recommend that your resignation be honored."

Mapledent inclined his head. "I appreciate that."

He turned and walked away. "Are you coming, Farrington?"

"No," Howie said.

Mapledent completed his exit in solitude, passing Billy as he left.

Billy, hair wet, and attired in a large, blazing white, terry cloth robe, completed what was left of the Committee. "What was that all about?"

"Damned if I know," Julia said. "Bea said we were moving the Committee meetings to LIT until the mayhem at Cabot House stopped and Mapledent got mad and resigned."

Billy turned to Howie, "Do you have any idea why he got mad? Does the rest of DRA think he's screwy?"

Howie shrugged. "I haven't been in Washington long enough to know. I, personally, would vote for screwy. I've seen other misogynists in the organization and other power-mad nuts, but never anything like him."

"G. Douglas notwithstanding," I said, "next Tuesday, two o'clock at LIT. We'll miss the nourishment at Cabot House, but I think we can manage to come up with coffee and doughnuts. I'll go tell Mr. Hamilton that we'll be back when whatever is going on is stopped. Assuming that he'll have us back."

I found his office, tapped on his door, and entered at his "Come in."

I explained that we would move the meetings elsewhere until we were sure that it was safe to return.

He smiled at me. "I quite understand. I hope that you don't feel that Cabot House was at fault in any way."

"Cabot House at fault? Of course not. That would be totally unreasonable. We could not have been treated better anywhere."

His smile broadened. "'Unreasonable' is not usually a deterrent to the complaints of some of our guests. I hope we'll see you again as soon as this unfortunate mess gets cleared up." He rose and we shook on it.

I went back to the group and we mulled over Mapledent's behavior until a staff member arrived to let us know that Billy's clothes were clean, dry, and wearable. Julia and I went to our sitting rooms and swapped our waders for real shoes while Billy repaired to his sitting room and dressed. Then we all got in the clunker and drove to DoTI. I dropped my passengers off and returned to LIT. Patted the Mustang on its cute convertible top as I walked past it.

I finished dealing with the detritus on my desk and called Alex.

"Are you ready to go home already?" he asked.

"No. But you wouldn't believe what happened at Cabot House. I'm going to brief Pie and thought you might want to hear the first recounting."

"Okay. I'll meet you in Pie's office."

I stopped at Jean's office to make sure that things were running smoothly and continued my journey toward Pie's.

Lenore said, "Dr. Pie's wife is in with him, Bea."

"That's good. I love the woman."

Pie's door was slightly ajar. As I approached, Bessie was saying, "It's a real shame that Bea lost the baby in that auto crash. She'd have made a wonderful mother."

I froze.

Pie said, "I know. I talked with Jim Daly. He can't say enough about how Bea treats his daughter."

I turned away from the door and into Alex who had come up behind me. We walked back to my office. I closed the door and leaned up against the doorjamb. Alex put his hands on my shoulders and I moved into his arms and he held me close.

"Hon, do you want to adopt a kid?"

I moved away slightly. "No, not unless you do. If you want to we can. I'd love the child."

"No," Alex said. "I would only want to adopt if you really wanted a child. Do you?"

"No. I really wanted to have a child with Harry. And I would love to carry and raise your child. But to have a child just to have a child, no. I know that's not reasonable. There's a moral imperative that says that we should adopt a kid who needs a home. But I don't feel that I *need* a child and unless *you* need a child, I don't think it's the right thing to do. Can you understand that?"

Alex kissed the top of my head. "No. I can't understand that, even though I feel exactly the same way. We'll just have to live our lives not understanding one another or ourselves. Are you ready to go to Pie's?"

"Hold me for just another minute."

He did so.

Alex said, "I never believed it was possible to love someone as much as I love you."

I said, "I have no words to express my love. How did we get so lucky?"

We left my office and walked down to Pie's.

Bessie got up and kissed Alex and me, in that order. "So how was your Committee meeting, Bea?"

I sat down. "You wouldn't believe..."

"*Oy!*" said my boss. "Not another one."

"Complete with leeches and sound effects." I described the whole scene, including Billy heroically carrying the wounded woman up to Cabot House.

"So someone just pitched her into the marsh and left her there to die or not die, as the case may be?" Alex asked.

"It would seem that way," I answered.

"What kind of a monster..." Bessie began and then stopped.

"No kind of a monster that I'm acquainted with," I said. "The ambulance took her to Maryland General where, presumably, they tended to the leeches and her leg. I'll visit her tomorrow."

Pie asked, "What was Mapledent's reaction?"

"Completely inexplicable. First, he apologized for his past behavior and was wonderfully cooperative. Then I told what was left of the Committee that we'd have future meetings here at LIT until we found out what was going on and stopped it."

Pie cut in, "Good move."

"Obvious move," I said. "but Mapledent objected. Said we shouldn't have the meetings at LIT because he didn't want to drive this far.   But LIT's closer to him than is Cabot House and we're right in between Julia and him.

"Logic did not convince the fool and he resigned.   Assuming that DRA accepts his resignation, no more G. Douglas."

"And the oboe is clearly understood," quoted Bessie.

"As an ill wind," continued Alex.

"That no one blows good." Pie finished.

On that note Alex and I left the office and headed toward Alexandria.

It was a lovely, top-down evening. In tribute, I burst into song.

Me: As someday it may happen that a damnfool must be found

　　　I've got a little list

Alex: She's got a little list

Me: The most repulsive of the group where all damnfools abound

　　　At the forefront of my list

　　　Is that dolt misogynist

Alex: He never will be missed

　　　He never will be missed

I turned to Alex.   "Do you think you could learn to play a kazoo?"

He glared at me, outraged.   Then burst out laughing.   "Boy, did I ever have that coming."

We stopped at the grocery store and picked up Buddy and his offerings of salad and wine.   He grabbed a baguette on the way out of the store.   Making friends with your grocer is a good thing to do.

The salad was wonderful, with big chunks of feta mixed with the greens.   The wine was a Sicilian nero d'avola.   That grape was, Buddy informed us, indigenous to Sicily.   Most of them are used as blending

grapes, but recently they have started being cultivated for their own sake.
The one Buddy brought was the perfect choice for the beef stew.
Definitely not screw top.

As we were finishing up the meal, Buddy informed us that he had
met The Girl. The Most Wonderful Girl in the World. He wondered if
we would consider inviting both him and The Girl for dinner some time,
maybe next month. We thought that was a lovely idea. We had cookies
for dessert. Of course.

Some time, near the end of dinner, I had begun to feel a bit queasy.
By the time I finished a cookie, I was good and sick. I left the bathroom
and told Alex and Buddy that I thought something was definitely not right.

The emergency room at Alexandria General beckoned. Alex and I
took the Mustang, Buddy following in case he was needed. Fortunately, it
was a slow night and shortly I was plunked on one of the curtained cots.
Or maybe it wasn't a slow night and the staff was just tired of me throwing
up all over their hospital floor. Whatever.

The nurses took blood and in no time at all, a very good looking
Indian doctor popped into my cubicle. "What have you been eating?"

I described dinner.

"Was anyone else sick?"

"Not that I know of. But the other two diners are here. They
seem okay."

"When did you have dinner?"

"Just before I arrived here."

"What did you eat, say, six or seven hours ago?"

I described lunch. "...egg salad, shrimp, and mushroom
sandwiches..."

"Mushroom sandwiches?"

"Among all the other things."

The man looked worried. "Here's the deal. The blood tests show that you've got a problem with your liver. Typical of mushroom, at this time of year probably amanita, poisoning. I'm going to get you some liquid charcoal to swallow. Swallow it. Then I'm going to put you in a hospital bed and get you some more liquid charcoal to swallow. This will be repeated over and over again for the entire night and part of the day. The liquid charcoal tastes terrible. You will be tempted not to take it. But remember, if you do not take it, most likely you will die. Do you understand?"

"Yes," I said, "you have certainly caught my attention."

The first dose of liquid charcoal arrived. The good doctor was correct. It tasted terrible. Then I was wheeled upstairs, with Alex and Buddy trailing behind the guerny.

Buddy volunteered to return to our house and bring me some clothes. We took him up on the offer.

Alex remained in the room with me, holding my hand.

"Alex," I said, "I think you should call Cabot House and ask Mr. Hamilton to warn the staff about the mushroom sandwiches. And see if you can get hold of Julia, Billie, Howie, and Doug. If they're feeling ill they should get to the hospital right away."

Alex picked up the phone and started making calls.

Another dose of charcoal arrived.

Alex finished making the calls. "Everyone seems to be okay except Mapledent. I talked to his wife – he had been throwing up and went to the emergency room. Wouldn't let her go with him. She hasn't heard from him yet."

Buddy came back with some clean clothes and a bag for my dirty clothes. W e told him to go home. I'd survive the mushrooms, if not the charcoal, and he needed to get some sleep before opening the store the next day. He kissed me good-bye and left.

I had been put into a double room. My roommate, who weakly greeted me when I arrived, looked startlingly like the pig in *Alice in Wonderland* – or was it *Through the Looking Glass*? O ne of them. A nd she snuffled. She snuffled when she was awake and she snuffled when she was asleep. But it wasn't a continuous snuffle. She'd snuffle for a while and then she'd stop. Alex and I would start to doze and she'd start again, waking us up. Between the snuffles, the charcoal, and the occasional blood test, we didn't get much sleep.

About eight in the morning, Pie and Bessie arrived. They had lied, telling the staff nurse that they were my adoptive parents. They were such a distinguished looking pair that the nurse believed them. She told them that I wasn't out of the woods yet but that it was looking good.

Alex called Mapledent's wife. She told him that he was at Good Samaritan Hospital but was about to be released. He was okay.

At eleven o'clock I was given my last dose of charcoal and at noon the doctor came into the room and bade me farewell.

I was feeling surprisingly good. Buddy had brought me clean clothes and after consultation with my sleepy husband, we decided to go to LIT. Alex was looking a little grubby, but given the usual garb of his terminal scientists, no one would notice.

CHAPTER 10

May 29 (cont.), 1992

Arriving at LIT about one o'clock, I found Bessie in my office.

"What a nice surprise!" I said.

She kissed me. "I had the feeling you'd be silly enough to come to the office straight from the hospital. I wanted to talk with you."

"That sounds ominous. What's wrong?"

"We thought we heard someone outside Pie's door yesterday. We asked Lenore. She said you were there and left. Did you overhear Pie and me talking about you?"

"Yes. Yes, I did."

"I'm sorry, Bea. You know we would never intentionally say or do anything to hurt you."

"I know that."

Bessie produced a half-smile. "You may have noticed that Pie and I are childless."

"That has come to my attention." I returned the half-smile.

"We didn't want children," she said. "We both have rewarding careers and either our careers would have been neglected or our children would have been neglected. Neither were appetizing alternatives. We've never regretted the decision to remain childless."

"We wanted you to know that it was possible to have a good marriage and a good life without children."

Bessie observed that my eyes were tearing up. "*Ach*," she said, I've upset you and that was the last thing I wanted to do."

"That's okay." A thought occurred to me. I tried to suppress a grin.

"What's so funny?" Bessie demanded.

With that, I started to laugh out loud. "Do you remember that old Abbott and Costello routine? Niagara Falls?"

Bessie stared at me. "You mean the one where Costello's jail mate goes nuts every time he hears the words 'Niagara Falls'? Where he says 'Slowly I turned' and starts whacking away at Costello?"

"That one. Do you think that eventually, every time I hear the word 'Baby' I'll say, 'Slowly I turned...'"

Bessie said, "You're impossible!" and *she* started to laugh.

We embraced. We were standing there with our arms around one another, laughing helplessly, when Pie walked in.

He observed us for a minute and then announced, "You're both impossible!" Which caused further gales of laughter.

Eventually we all sat soberly down.

"Bessie," Pie said, "did you tell Bea about the bones?"

"Not yet." She turned to me. "The Smithsonian wanted me to take a look at some artifacts a *gonif* was trying to sell them. So I didn't get to Sam's bones until late yesterday. It's the skeleton of a male, about five feet tall, probably somewhere in his thirties, give or take a year or two. No identifying marks, no old broken bones – nothing obvious like that. I can't tell anything else without a more thorough look at the skeleton."

"Have you told Sam?"

"I called him last night."

"I'll call him this morning," I said. "The skeleton could be that of a botanist who didn't show up for a lecture he was to give.

"What happened with the Smithsonian's artifacts?"

"They were fakes," Bessie said, "which is fortunate for the *gonif*. If they had been real, he would have had to explain how he came into possession of an Egyptian national treasure. Penalty for that is a lot more serious than trying to sell the Brooklyn Bridge to the Smithsonian.

"The Smithsonian normally wouldn't have asked me to look at the stuff, but their experts are all off at a conference and since I was handy, I got tapped.

"Sam's bones are locked in our car trunk."

She and Pie got up. "What time will we see you tomorrow?"

I responded, "Chuck's pre-opening gala starts around eleven. Why don't we all meet at your house at ten? Will Don and Connie join us?"

"Unfortunately, no," Pie said. "They had a prior commitment. So I think it will just be Bessie, me, you, Alex, Jim Daly and his kid."

"Her name is Chrissie."

"Thank you. I did not want to spend the day calling her 'Jim's kid'."

"Maybe you should come a little early," Bessie said. "Nine instead of ten, and have breakfast at our house before we go."

"Did you bring a recipe back from Ecuador?"

"No. Actually, it's from the Middle East. Do you remember that apple place on the way to Hamburgers And? The one that has double yolk eggs."

I admitted that I not only remembered it, but had partaken of the eggs.

"Well," Bessie concluded, "the recipe can take the double yolks. Can you come that early?"

"Easily. This is one of our alpaca farm nights – we're close by. Should I ask Jim and Chrissie, too?"

"Of course."

They took leave of my office.

I picked up the phone and called Sheriff Sam. I caught him just as he was about to leave for a patrol of his domain.

"Sam, I just talked with Bessie. Her description of the bones resembles a missing botanist from Georgetown University. His name is Craig Thibodeau. Georgetown should have enough information to locate him."

"Now how on earth would you know that?"

"Howie Farrington told me. A five foot botanist didn't show up to give a lecture. Howie said that if the skeleton didn't turn out to be Petey, it might be Thibodeau."

"Thank you, ma'am. I'll call them right away and let you know what we find.

"Where are the bones now?"

"They're locked in Bessie's car trunk."

"Is the car at LIT?"

"Sure."

"Would you tell Bessie that I'm sending a deputy to pick them up. He'll give her a receipt."

"Will do. But don't hang up. In all the excitement I forgot to ask you about the snake man. Did he show you the note?"

"Yeah. No joy. Printed on a big post-it. No fingerprints. No way of knowing who put him up to it."

"Nuts. I can make a good guess but guesses don't butter any parsnips."

"Anything you want us to do?"

"Nothing you can do. But thanks for everything."

"We serve and protect."

Sam rang off.

I let Bessie know that a deputy would come calling and walked over to the Biology Center to check on Chrissie. She was taking turns with Ralph, looking through a microscope. She looked up when she heard me approach.

"Hi, Dr. Goode."

"Hello, Chrissie, don't let me disturb you."

Ralph looked up. He smiled. "Do you have any more at home like her?"

"Not that I know of. I'll look in the closet."

Ralph laughed and returned to the microscope.

"Chrissie, we're going to meet at Pie's tomorrow at nine for breakfast. I'll give your dad directions."

"Thank you."

Chrissie looked as if she wanted to get back to Ralph and the microscope so I left, waving good-bye to Molly, who was hovering in the vicinity.

When I got back to my office, I called Jim and gave him directions to Pie's.

Bessie and Pie live in a small house in the country, fairly close to LIT. It has the appearance of being isolated without actually *being* isolated. They were close enough to Bella Villa to be able to pick up basics when they ran out, close enough to LIT so that Pie doesn't have much of a commute, close enough to the Baltimore-Washington airport to be convenient when Bessie was on her way to or from a dig, and close enough to Washington to have a cultural life when the mood struck them. They had remodeled the place immediately after they bought it, so that Bessie could cook up her usual storm when she was in town. She is a great cook and they had remodeled the kitchen to accommodate her greatness. Altogether a satisfactory abode. Its only drawback is that it's hard to find. Despite my painstaking directions, Jim would probably go back and forth, passing Pie's driveway several times, before he noticed it, hidden under the oaks.

Next phone call was to Maryland General Hospital to check on Emmaline. She was no longer there. Where did she go? No information. Was she okay? No information. Could I speak to her doctor? Patient privacy. Frustrated, I hung up and made a start on my in-box.

Jeanne Cameron walked into my office just as I was making a dent (albeit small) in my paperwork. "You'll never guess who just called me," she said.

"Anyone I know?"

"Ethel the Useless. She wants to return to LIT."

Ethel was a former employee who was – to put it mildly – somewhat less than satisfactory. She had filed an Equal Employment Opportunities suit against LIT (it had been thrown out), had laced my cupcake (which she, herself, inadvertently swallowed) with ipecac, called a visiting group of disabled students 'retards,' refused to order kosher airline meals for a traveling Orthodox Jewish computer scientist, and edited a Biology Center paper to the point where it was unpublishable.

"What did she want you to do about it?"

Jeanne giggled. "She wanted me to intercede with you so that you would tell Human Relations to let you hire her.

"What should I tell her?"

"Uh, tell her that we don't have any slots at present, but should a slot come open, I'll put her on my list of people to hire." *I've got a little list.*

"You will?"

"Yeah. Just behind Jeffrey Dahmer."

"Well, maybe I won't talk about the list." She laughed and left.

The next phone call was from Howie Farrington.

"Hey, Bea. The forms to upgrade me to a GS-15 are being processed and while that's happening, I'm in charge of choosing the DRA people for the Committee."

"That is marvelous news. I think we might be able to get something accomplished.

"By the way, I called the hospital. They told me that Emmaline checked out but wouldn't tell me anything else. What are you going to do about her?"

"I don't have to do anything. She called Mapledent, who bucked it to me. She not only resigned from the Committee, she resigned from DRA. Her parents picked her up at the hospital and brought her home. She doesn't want anything more to do with us Godless heathens.

"In case you were wondering, I'm not Godless. I can say 'Hallelujah' with the best of the brethren."

I'm going to enjoy working with Howie.

I asked, "Have you picked your colleagues for the Committee?"

"Not yet. Do you have someone you think would be good?"

"No, but I think Julia knows some capable women. Call her if you like. Unless you'd rather I do it."

"I can do it," Howie said. "I'll see what her candidate's discipline

126

is and then fill in the blank.   I'm new at headquarters, but I know a lot of the people here."

I provided Julia's contact number. "Congratulations on the promotion.   I guess it was worth a poke on the nose."

Howie laughed.   "I'll forever be grateful to Drumm."

I settled down with paperwork and dozed off.   When I awoke, the papers seemed to have multiplied while I was gone. *Did they mate?*

Sam called around four.   Craig Thibodeau had not appeared to teach his afternoon classes.   After some checking and more than a few bureaucratic obstructions, he was finally given Thibodeau's 'in case of emergency' number.   He was living in a rented flat – the number was that of his landlord.   Sam contacted the landlord and received the information that Thibodeau had no living relatives.   The landlord didn't have the name of Thibodeau's dentist, but furnished that of his doctor.   The doctor confirmed that Thibodeau had no living relatives.   He also provided the name of the man's dentist.   Joe was, at the moment, bringing the skull to the dentist to compare with x-rays.   "I'll be surprised," said Sam, "if they don't match. How many missing five foot guys in their thirties are there? I'll call you as soon as we know for sure."

I asked him, "Are you going to the pre-opening of Chuck's museum?'

"Of course.   How else will the peace be maintained?"

"Bessie and Pie and two other people will be going with Alex and me.   We plan to have lunch at The Rabbit Hole.   Will you join us?"

"That would be an honor.   What time?"

"Eleven at the museum and lunch from there."

"I'll be there."   Sam disconnected.

He no sooner hung up than Julia called.   "Howie called and asked for a suggestion for a DRA Committee member. I recommended Shirley Cohen. She's a soil scientist."

"I remember her from your descriptions of capable, suitable women."

Julia sighed. "I felt like a crumb not recommending Marcy, but I don't think she's right for the Committee. Every time a vote went against her, she'd think she was being picked on."

We rang off.

I called Pie, updated him on the status of the Committee and then wandered down to Alex's office. It was tad early to leave for the farm, but I was sick and bug-eyed from paperwork. I'm a lousy bureaucrat.

Alex finished what he was doing. "Where do you want to eat?"

There weren't a lot of choices. The Rabbit Hole was one. The other was Hamburgers And. Since we were going to eat at The Rabbit Hole the next day, I aimed the Mustang at Hamburgers And.

Hamburgers And was a loony restaurant in the opposite direction from Bella Villa and Alexandria. Turning left out of the parking lot, we went farther up the mountain – big hill, really – past the Observatory, DRA, a Pumpkin Shoot, and the orchard where they sold apples and double-yolk eggs. Then down the other side where we came to the town that hosted Hamburgers And. We didn't know the name of the town, we just referred to it as No-Name. There wasn't a Welcome sign and no town name adorned any of the few buildings on the main street. It was a bedraggled little town containing a few discouraged stores and Hamburgers And – its only excuse for existence. There were always at least a dozen cars in the lot, owned by nearby farmers, we surmised. I pulled into the lot and we entered the rustic dining room of Hamburgers

And. The walls were log, the lighting dim.

We found a booth and sat down.   There was a large board on the wall, displaying the names of the accessories available to top off the hamburgers. The accessories included onions, tomatoes, lettuce, ketchup, mustard, barbeque sauce, six varieties of cheese, pickles, chili peppers, mayo, slaw, bacon, avocado, fried egg, and mushrooms. That was the total menu and no matter what or how many you ordered as toppings, your hamburger cost nine dollars.   The waitress came over and plunked two glasses of water on our table.   "You want your burgers cooked the usual way?"

We allowed as how medium rare still suited us.

"Whaddya want on them."

Alex ordered bacon, mushrooms, and barbecue sauce. I opted for cheddar, tomatoes, and onion. Mushrooms didn't appeal to me.   We both ordered a Sam Adams beer.

Before she could escape, I asked the waitress, "What's the name of this town?"

She looked at me in astonishment.   "You been coming in here for about a year and you never read the sign where you entered town?"

Alex said, "There is no sign."

The waitress turned to me. "Is that right?"

"That's right."

"Well, there used to be a sign."

With that, she returned to the kitchen.

By this time, the restaurant was filling up and when our orders were ready the now-harried waitress slapped our burgers on the table and scurried off.

We ate our burgers, drank our beer, and left for the farm.   We still don't know the name of the town.

CHAPTER 11

May 30, 1992

During the four days that we were tending to business, two baby alpacas (called 'crias') were born. While Alex was giving Gertie her good-bye smooches and farewell apple slices, I watched the little guys frolicking. They're amazing. As soon as they're born they get up on their four legs, wobble a bit, get steady, walk under mama, help themselves to the buffet, and frisk. That's it. The only other thing for them to do is eat and grow.

Chuck was going to have a fine day for his pre-opening festivities. The sky was blue. The sun was shining. The Mustang's top was down and all was well with the world.

I was motoring up the long, dirt driveway that led to the Lee home when I noticed Jim's car following me. He and Chrissie were laughing as they got out of the car. "If Daddy hadn't seen you pull in," Chrissie said, "we'd still be driving back and forth. Why didn't you tell us the driveway was hidden by foliage?"

"I did."

"You said oaks. Those are hickories."

"I'm management. I'm not expected to know specifics."

Pie answered our knock. "Good. You're all here." He led us into the living room. "Bessie's in the kitchen, making breakfast. Do you want coffee while you wait?"

We did. Pie disappeared.

Alex and I had been in the room so often that we had forgotten the effect it had on first-time visitors. It contained an amazing assortment of artifacts and furniture that Bessie had accumulated in her thirty five years of travel. In addition to the antique furniture (of the sturdy kind), the collection also included a skeleton, which peeked out from behind a bookcase. It was somewhat unnerving. Pie had added to the decor with a series of framed pictures of microbiological wonders. I was partial to *Purple nonsulfur bacterium Rhodobacter ferrooxidans*. Chrissie, however, found more to admire in *Aedes albopictus*. Ah well, her taste would develop as she matured.

Pie returned with a tray of coffee cups and saucers. He put them on a table carved from a fossilized something and disappeared again, shortly to return with another tray holding a large pot of coffee, sugar, and cream. "I'm going to help Bess in the kitchen. I'll come get you when breakfast is served."

Jim asked, "What's the story with Hadaman's museum? I thought he was in charge of facilities at DoTI."

"He is," Alex responded. "But he has a whole different life outside of the Department. He lives in Bella Villa and he makes metal, I guess you'd call them, sculptures, for the Homecoming Parade every year. He's done eight or nine of them, and the town decided to put them in a museum.

"The museum will officially open next week, but they're having a pre-opening for Chuck's friends and other notables. We'll take you to The Rabbit Hole after we've finished gawking."

"The rabbit hole?" asked Chrissie. "What rabbit hole?"

"It's a restaurant," I informed her. "They make Welsh rabbits."

"Is that like a Welsh rarebit?"

Alex and I frowned at her. Alex stated, "There is no such thing as a Welsh rarebit. The proper term is Welsh rabbit."

I added, "Indeed, the 1926 edition of Fowler's *Dictionary of Modern English Usage* states categorically that 'Welsh Rabbit is amusing and right. Welsh Rarebit is stupid and wrong.' Do you presume, young woman, to argue with Fowler?"

"Oh, no no," Chrissie responded, "Rather I would be put on a stool and dunked until I drowned than argue with Fowler."

She turned to Jim. "Daddy, who the heck is Fowler?"

Alex can be forgiven for laughing and spewing coffee all over Bessie's fossilized table. He was hurriedly mopping up when Pie came in to announce that breakfast was served.

Bessie had made shakshuka. This is an Israeli dish of eggs poached in a very spicy tomato sauce. The double yolk eggs added a particularly elegant touch. The sauce is a mixture of garlic, onion, tomato, feta cheese, and most of the spices known to the modern world. She served it with pitas, for dipping.

Not too shabby for a world-renowned archeologist.

Over breakfast, Pie asked me, "Have you told Jim and Chrissie about the turmoil on your Committee?"

Jim and Chrissie looked up, interested.

"Not yet. For no other reason than that there hasn't been an opportunity."

I proceeded to tell them.

"You mean," said Jim, "that one person has been murdered and another person has been thrown into a bucket of leeches?"

"I wouldn't exactly call the marsh a 'bucket,' but other than that, you're right on."

"Geez," Chrissie said, "and you told us to bring waders so that we can explore that same marsh?"

Alex laughed. "I don't think a crazed axe murderer is going to attack a group of six people. And even if he does, he'll only get a couple of us before he's stopped."

"*Genug*," Pie said. "I shouldn't have brought it up while we're eating."

We stopped talking and mopped up the last of the shakshuka.

Bessie told us not to clear the table – someone had been hired to come in and clean up after us. That might even have been true.

We arranged ourselves in Pie's Taurus and headed toward Bella Villa. Jim and Chrissie had never been to Bella Villa. So, since we were a little early, we cruised Main Street in order to show them the sights. Unlike No-Name village, Bella Villa looked as if the residents cared about their town. Aside from one decrepit bar, every building on the street had a fresh coat of paint. There was a general store that stocked dry goods, sundries, a selection of   meat and in-season groceries. A second hand store did double duty as a pawn shop.   A pet shop took care of a few rescue dogs as well as selling some hand-made accouterments for dogs and cats.   There was also Petrofsky's hardware store where Petey stayed when he wasn't getting himself lost, and a tattoo parlor. I don't know how the tattoo parlor stayed in business.   I never saw anyone in Bella Villa sporting its art. And of course, there was The Rabbit Hole.   It's an inviting little town.

The village green, which ran alongside Main Street, was anchored at one end by the bandstand and at the other end by city hall.   The jail, the police station and the sheriff's office shared a square brick building to the right of city hall.   To the left of city hall was Chuck's new museum.

Formerly the town's visitor information center, it was an attractive wooden structure painted a glossy navy blue. Chuck had fabricated a seven foot metal llama, which graced the entrance to the museum. Metal steps invited kids to climb up to the back of the llama and a metal slide invited them to skid back down the other side. The sculpture was overrun with kids.

We found a place to park and entered the museum. Chuck was at the far end of the museum showing Sam and a few of his deputies the sights.

"Wow," said Chrissie, the college sophomore. "Is that gorgeous hunk Chuck Hadaman?"

"Down, Chrissie," I said. "He's gay."

"That big, beautiful guy is gay?"

"He is that," Alex affirmed.

"Nuts!" Chrissie bemoaned.

"Never mind," Jim said. "He's too old for you, anyway."

Chuck, Sam, and Joe ambled up. Bessie and I got pecks on the cheek from each of them. I introduced them to the two strangers in the group. and Chuck offered to take us on the guided tour.

The building's interior had been remodeled, replastered and repainted with cream colored walls. Soft florescent lighting shone through a stiff translucent plastic lens, which covered the entire ceiling area. The floor was hardwood oak. Chuck told us that the work and the materials had all been donated.

Scattered about the room were nine sizeable transparent cubes set on brushed steel legs. Each cube contained one of Chuck's fabrications. We moved as a group from cube to cube.

The earliest cube contained the first one Chuck had made, in 1983.

That one and the next were concocted before the contest was instituted. They were simpler than those that followed, since one of the aims of the contest was to stump Hadaman.

Cube 1 contained three cheerleaders. Pressing the activation button on the cube caused the cheerleaders to wave their pom poms and jump into the air.

Cube 2 contained a wide receiver. Pressing the activation button caused a football to drop out of the air, the receiver to jump and catch it.

Cube 3 contained a kicker and a goalpost. Pressing the activation button caused the kicker to kick a football, which hits the crossbar and the entire goalpost falls down.

Cube 4 contained six bicyclists, dressed in football gear. Pressing the activation button causes five of the bikers to follow the lead biker, who steers the whole group around the goalposts at each end of the football field. Bistro lights are wrapped around each bike's wheels. The lights get brighter as the bikes make a turn, fade on the straight-away. The bikers sing Manfred Mann's "Blinded by the Light".

Cube 5 contained two defensive linemen, a quarterback, and a referee. Pressing the activation button caused the linemen to run toward the quarterback, sandwich the referee, and knock him on his patooty.

Cube 6 contained one female and nine male cheerleaders. Pressing the activation button caused four male cheerleaders to come forward, three male cheerleaders to jump on their shoulders, two male cheerleaders to jump on *their* shoulders, the female cheerleader to jump on *their* shoulders and the pyramid to collapse.

Cube 7 contained a quarterback, a receiver, a goalpost, and behind the goalpost, the band. Pressing the activation button caused the quarterback to overthrow the receiver and the football to land in the tuba.

Cube 8 had last year's offering – a football player chasing a pig. The activation button caused the football player's arms and legs to pump and the pig to squeal.

Cube 9 was empty, awaiting this year's winner.

It was an astonishing show.

Chuck went off to greet some arriving visitors while our group dispersed, wandering around, reactivating our favorites. One of Sam's deputies had been dispatched to sit behind a sleek desk situated to the left of the door. Looseleaf books, each page containing a color picture of a fabrication, were being sold for ten bucks. The deputy explained that the books were in looseleaf form so that single pages could be bought and added each year. We bought one book per couple.

When we finally completed our playing and our purchasing, we headed off for lunch at The Rabbit Hole, Sam trailing behind in his cruiser.

The decor of The Rabbit Hole was a tribute to the name. Rabbits were everywhere. Hanging from the ceiling. Sitting on the tables. Peeking out of the kitchen. There was even one six foot Harvey-type rabbit, fabricated by Chuck, which sat next to the door. It nodded and squeaked every time someone entered. Jim and Chrissie were entranced.

As we settled ourselves in, Duane, the proprietor, maitre d', and waiter came over to take our order. "Where's Chuck?

I said, "He's hosting the pre-opening of the museum."

"Ah," said Duane, "sure. You all want rabbits?"

We all wanted rabbits.

"You all want a glass of Bud?" He looked at Sheriff Sam and then at Chrissie. "Are you twenty one?"

"Almost," Chrissie said.

Duane looked at Sam again. "Well," he said, "with the sheriff sitting right here, 'almost' ain't good enough." He trotted off.

While we were waiting for the rabbits, Sam informed us that the skull's teeth were a match. The skeleton was what remained of Craig Thibodeau. "We haven't had time to do much of an investigation," Sam said, "but he doesn't seem to be the kind of man who would make enemies. He lived alone in a rented flat, didn't make noise, paid his rent on time. From what we've learned so far, his colleagues all liked him; he didn't have a girl friend. He was kind of an innocuous guy."

Our Welsh rabbits and beer arrived and we addressed them with the respect they deserved.

Pie explained to Sam that we were going to see the Cabot House wetland. "Do you want to join us?"

"Sure," Sam said. "This is not a duty day for me. What route do you plan to take to get there?"

Pie looked puzzled. "What do you mean? We'll go through town and turn right at the Cabot House sign."

"There's a better way. If we pass the sign and go up to the next road, turn right for about a half mile, we can park on the verge and go down the slope to the ferns and get to the wetland. That way we won't have to disturb the people at Cabot House. I can take the cruiser and lead you there."

He turned to Bessie. "Will you be all right going down the slope?"

Bessie gave him the fish eye. "I just came back from a month exploring the Andes. Are you asking me if I can walk down a hill?"

Sam looked abashed. "Sorry about that, Bessie."

Then he said, "I'd better call Cabot House and tell them we'll be on the grounds. With all that's been going on in their wetland, they might think we're up to mischief and call the sheriff."

Alex picked up the check, Pie protested, Sam made the call, and we went off to the wetland.

CHAPTER 12

May 30 (cont.) and May 31, 1992

We followed Sam's cruiser out of the parking lot, past the Cabot House turnoff, and turned right onto a narrow country road. Presumably the road where the school teacher was killed. Shortly, the road widened to accommodate a grassy verge. Sam signaled and we pulled over onto the grass, behind a parked Jeep and a Toyota pick-up. Their owners were nowhere in sight. Sam got out of the cruiser carrying a "County Sheriff" placard, which he placed on the Taurus's windshield. "I don't think the Staties patrol this road," he said, "but in case they do, this'll protect you from tickets and other nasty things."

Sam, who was wearing his uniform boots, didn't need waders. But the rest of us hopped up and down getting them on. Chrissie's waders, hand-me-downs from her mother, were a bit too big for her, but serviceable.

"We ready?" Sam asked. We were.

"Follow me."

Sam led us through a gap in the trees and about halfway down the slope, when Pie called, "Wait a minute."

We stopped. The ground under the trees was covered with small white flowers. Hundreds of them. Pie was kneeling down, oblivious to the mess the ground was making of his perfectly creased pants.

"I'm no botanist," Pie said, "but these look like small white lady's slippers." He turned to Chrissie. "Can you identify them?"

"Not really," she said. "But I remember my botany teacher

140

showing us similar pictures and saying they were practically extinct."

"Hey," Jim called, "there are holes here – it appears that someone has been digging them up."

Alex joined the forum. "Look here. There's some bare ground where it looks like a whole layer of them have been removed."

Bessie said, "This is bad. The rest of these have to be protected. Who owns this land?"

Sam said, "I think it belongs to Cabot House. What's so special about these flowers?"

Pie said, "Lady's slippers are orchids. If Chrissie and I are correct, this variety is the small, white, lady's slipper. It's an especially rare and endangered species. It looks as if someone discovered this patch of them and is trying to dig them up."

"Why?"

"To sell them," Bessie said. "They're like any other rare thing. There's a market for them. Orchids especially attract collectors. They discovered a rare lady's slipper in England – rarer than this one. They think it's the last one left in the UK. They've put a round-the-clock police guard over it."

"But how high could the market price go for a flower?" Alex asked.

Bessie answered, "The Brits estimated that a cutting from the plant would sell for about five thousand pounds."[*]

We stood in stunned silence.

Finally Pie said, "I think this explains a lot about Mapledent's behavior. I think he got on the Committee and stayed on it to prevent people from going up the slope. This must be his private source of

---

[*] See *London Daily Mail*, 7 May 2010.

income."

I nodded. "And when I moved the meetings to LIT, he stopped worrying about the Committee going up the slope, so he picked a fight and resigned.

"I'll bet Drumm is in on it. He must have smacked Howie to divert him from walking up the slope. And it's a beagle to a bagel that G. Douglas's cooperative activities lasted just long enough to poison my mushroom sandwich. That smarmy louse."

Alex said, "But he got sick, too."

"He's a botanist," I said. "He's not a mycologist but he certainly knows something about mushrooms. He must have given himself a very slight dose of amanita or some other poisonous spring mushroom. Enough to make him sick and divert suspicion, but not enough to kill him." I thought for a minute. "Or more likely, he just swallowed a harmless emetic, threw up a few times for his wife's benefit, and then pretended to go to the hospital."

Jim said, "But why would he want to kill you? What good would that do him?"

I responded, "Probably his justification was that if he got rid of me, he would assume the chair of the committee and could find some reason to bar the members from climbing the slope. But my guess is that the real reason is that he dislikes me intensely. After all, I'm one of those despised she-creatures and when the bureaucratic in-fighting occurred, the she-creature whipped his *tuches*."

Alex added, "Good chance that he killed that biology teacher. The poor woman probably stopped to see what was in the woods and picked up a leaf to show her class."

Sam brought some sense to the conversation. "Good theory. Do you have any evidence?"

"Not a scintilla," Pie confessed.

"Well," Sam said, "let's continue down and see what develops. I'll radio for a deputy to come keep an eye on the place until we make sure that these are the plants you think they are. If they are, we'll decide what to do then. If Cabot House owns the land, they'll probably sign it over to a government agency. They don't use the land, they can't sell the plants, and they're being taxed. If the county owns it, we'll probably try to palm it off on the Feds."

As we walked down the slope, one of Chrissie's boots came off. I gave her my shoulder to lean on while she struggled to put it back on. No one else noticed and they continued on. We followed after.

Suddenly, there was a shout. "I'm a police officer. Drop that weapon. N ow!"

Through the trees we could see Sam, gun drawn. Mapledent was holding a raised sharpshooter. Someone was lying on the ground. Chrissie and I, hurrying, slipped and slid the rest of the way, landing at Mapledent's feet.

Chrissie stood up and Mapledent dropped the sharpshooter, grabbed her and shoved her in front of him, shielding himself from Sam's weapon.

Urbane as always, G. Douglas said, "Now, ladies and gentlemen, you all just stand where you are and I will leave with this lovely young lady. If you move, I will be compelled to break her neck."

Jim took a step. "If you hurt Chrissie, I'll kill you. Wherever you are, wherever you go, I'll kill you.'

Mapledent said, "In that case, I would appreciate it if you would forbear to take another step."

Chrissie, who did not appear to be at all shaken, said. "It's all right, Daddy. I can handle this."

And before another step could be taken or another word could be said, G. Douglas Mapledent had sailed over Chrissie's left shoulder and was lying on the ground. Thank God she hadn't signed up for golf.

It was then that we recognized the other man on the ground. Ronald Drumm. He was bleeding from a dreadful abdominal wound.

Jim ran to Chrissie. Sam handed the gun to Alex and told him to keep it trained on Mapledent while Sam radioed for help.

"If the son of a bitch moves, shoot him."

Pie, Bessie, and I knelt over Drumm, who was barely breathing.

Pie stripped off his shirt, and used it to keep the wound covered while Bessie and I applied pressure.

It seemed like hours, but it was actually less than five minutes before help came. Deputies ran from the direction of Cabot House. Emergency Medical Technicians ran down the hill, bearing a stretcher. Drumm was rushed to the ambulance. Sam instructed Joe to ride with them and record everything Drumm said. Mapledent was cuffed and herded into a cruiser.

It was all over.

At Dexter Hamilton's request, we met at Cabot House the next afternoon for lunch and the wrap-up of events. Elaine Ickes joined us. She was a tall, slim, beautifully groomed woman, probably in her mid-forties. I hope she becomes the next Secretary of DoTI. She'll deal well with Congress.

Over lunch, Sam began the briefing.

G. Douglas had lawyered up immediately and remained silent. The prosecutor's office had procured a search warrant and would examine his records. They would try to locate the collectors who had purchased lady's slippers from him.

Elaine asked, "If you do find some or all of them, will they admit to buying them from Mapledent?"

Sam thought about it. "I dunno. Depends on what kind of records Mapledent kept. I doubt if he intended to pay any income tax on the sales. I just don't know. Would any of the collectors ask for a receipt or would they just take the flowers and run? Search me.

"What I do know is that Drumm confessed all on the way to the hospital. Joe, bless him, actually had his recorder with him and not only taped Drumm's words but also took handwritten notes – witnessed and signed by the EMTs."

According to Drumm, Mapledent was the man who discovered the field of lady's slippers. Drumm was pretty sure that Mapledent was with the little botanist, Thibodeau, when the discovery was made and he almost certainly killed the little guy.

Once Thibodeau was out of the way, Mapledent went up to the field and was digging up the plants when Drumm, on a field trip, happened upon him. Drumm recognized the plants, realized what Mapledent was doing and, in return for keeping his mouth shut, got himself a piece of the action. This was about the time that the Committee was formed and Mapledent was chosen to head DRA's group.

"My guess," Sam went on, "is that he had lobbied for the assignment."

"Good guess," Elaine said. "The current DRA Secretary told Roger Biddle about the appointment and Roger told me that we were going to have to deal with a sexist moron."

She grinned. "And Bea did indeed deal with him."

She continued the narrative. "Mapledent put Drumm on the Committee and selected Farrington as the third member. Apparently he thought that Farrington, an agronomist new to headquarters, would be reasonably malleable and reasonably ignorant about flowers. The dastardly duo probably thought that, together, they could keep the DoTI Committee members off the slope."

I stuck my two cents in. "The first glitch popped up when Julia declared that she would take the DoTI members on a tour of their own. Since Mapledent couldn't control the tour, he must have dispatched Drumm to make sure that the DoTI team didn't enter the lady's slipper field. When Howie saw Drumm leave Cabot House, he decided to go along with him.

"I guess when the two of them reached the ferns, Howie wanted to go up the slope and the only way Drumm could think of to keep him from the climb was to start an argument. Julia immortalized on film the argument, which ended with the poke in the nose."

"That was my nose," Howie said, "and Drumm got kicked off the committee because of the poke. I feel honored to have sacrificed my schnozzola to the cause of justice."

"Yabbut," Julia said, "Mapledent replaced Drumm with that silly Emmaline Stutz. I suppose he thought she wouldn't make waves and even if she stumbled across the lady's slippers, she wouldn't know what she was seeing. Unfortunately for G. Douglas, she unintentionally did, in fact, make waves. She decided to go exploring around the wetland and got curious about the woods."

Sam said, "According to Drumm, he was on the slope digging up plants when he heard Stutz cry out. He had been using a hickory walking stick to help him maneuver around the hill and he was carrying it when he ran toward the sound. He recognized Stutz, realized that she was hurt, and used the walking stick to knock her out. He denied it, but we're pretty sure that if the blow hadn't knocked her out, he would have killed her. As it was, he picked up her limp body and chucked it into the marsh. He ran back up the slope, picked up the plants he had already dug up, covered his tracks as best he could, threw the plants into his pickup, and hightailed it out of there."

By that time, he realized that it was going to be impossible to keep people off the slope forever. So he returned with the kind of tools that would allow him to remove large clumps of plants at one time. He planned to dig up as many of them as would fit in the pickup. Mapledent could have whatever was left – if any *were* left. He was in the process of digging when Mapledent, who apparently also realized that he'd better dig while the digging was good, arrived at the slope and caught Drumm in the act."

What happened then was a kind of Errol Flynn-Basil Rathbone sharpshooter duel. As the two swashbucklers dueled down the slope, Drumm slipped and tumbled to the plateau where Mapledent ran him through. He was about to finish him off when Sam and the posse arrived.

Despite the best efforts of the emergency room staff, Drumm died within an hour of reaching the hospital.

"*Gottenyu!*" Pie muttered. "This can't be real."

"It's real enough," Sam said.

Elaine asked, "Will Mapledent get away with murdering Thibodeau?"

"Probably," Sam answered. "But there's no way he can avoid conviction for murdering Drumm. We all watched him try to finish the job."

In the event, Sam was right.

GLOSSARY OF YIDDISH WORDS AND PHRASES USED IN THIS BOOK

Bubele – darling, sweetie, a term of affection

Chazzer – pig, glutton

Genug – enough, sufficient

Geshvolen goen – puffed up genius

Gevalt – uh, oh, an expression of dismay

Gonif – thief

Gottenyu – dear God!

Kvetch – n. a complaint or gripe

           n. a person who continually complains or gripes

           v. to complain or gripe

Mishegoss - craziness

Nu – an all-purpose word that can mean anything from "how are you" doing" to "tell me". The English equivalent is "So?"

Oy – a disapproving sigh

Schmuck – a jerk

Shmegegge – a pain in the butt, a fool

Tuches – backside, bottom

Vos makhstu – how are you? what's going on?

EPILOGUE

Author's note: In 1992, Bea chaired the committee whose mandate was to investigate the effect of climate change on agriculture and the resultant effect on U.S. trade balance. I began to wonder whether the many domestic and international committees and agreements made any difference at all to the world's response to climate change.

I therefore decided to fast-forward twenty some years and take a look at what has happened in the intervening time. Pie and Bessie are now in their seventies. Alex and Bea are in their fifties. And the world is a couple of decades older.

The Cokers have retired to Florida where they are basking in the hurricane season. The alpaca farm is being run by some very pleasant tenants, overseen by Sandy and Daryl junior. Alex and Bea are still enjoying weekends and, in this year of the Sequester, weeks in the log cabin.

October 2013 - The Month of the Foolish Furlough

Alex gave Gretchen a kiss on the nose and an apple slice. She headed back to the herd and Alex headed to the Mustang. He slid into the driver's seat. "Is Gretch Gertie's granddaughter or great granddaughter?"

A weighty question which I gave the thought it deserved. "I dunno. Great granddaughter, I think. Maybe great great granddaughter."

Alex turned out of the driveway toward Pie's and Bessie's place. "Who else will be at dinner tonight?" he asked.

"Don and Connie and Elaine."

"What's Elaine doing with herself now?"

I said, "IBM lured her back with a big signing bonus and a meaningful vice presidency. She's been there until now, when Obama decided to split the Office of the Science Advisor in two and create the Office of the Technology Advisor. Elaine's going to head up that office."

Alex looked skeptical. "I suppose that's a response to the botched Affordable Care Act launch. Does Elaine know enough to get it fixed?"

"Well," I answered, "she came up through the ranks at IBM and if she's a tad rusty with the hands-on technologies, she sure ought to know what it takes to manage a complicated system."

Alex still looked skeptical, but with typical good grace he changed the subject.

"One of these years we ought to get a hybrid auto," he said, "if we're going to be good, environmentally sound citizens."

"Just as soon as our idiot governor and his legislature stop slapping a tax on the hybrids. I can't believe they did that."

I whined, "'We have to do it to make up for the lost gasoline revenue.' Imbeciles!"

Alex grinned. "Hey, I think they're on to something. We should tax all quadriplegics. They don't buy gasoline at all.

"By the way, my dear, do you remember when we used to stop for snoggles on the way to work?"

I gave him the look. "Since it was only a week ago, I think I might recall it."

Alex pulled over to the shoulder, unlatched his seatbelt, and grabbed me. A short snoggle later we were back on the road.

"Pie and Bessie just bought a Tesla," I told him.

"Really! Do you know how far it will go on a single charge?"

"Pie said between two and three hundred miles at fifty five miles an hour. Depends on how you drive and how big a battery you have. Pie and Bessie went top of the line, so they'll be closer to three hundred.

"Bessie said she was stopped at a red light and the guy in the car next to her opened his window and asked if her car was electric. When she nodded, he asked how many miles she got to the gallon."

Alex was still laughing when we pulled into Pie's driveway.

Don and Connie were getting out of their car as we drove up. We walked to the door together. Elaine greeted us. "Come on in. Pie and Bessie are in the kitchen."

We shed our coats and wandered into the living room.

"Where's Murray?" Connie looked around as if expecting Elaine's husband to appear from behind the skeleton.

Elaine laughed. "Overseas, trying to sell the Brooklyn Bridge to the Ukrainians. He'll be back next week."

We sat down. Elaine asked, "What are you going to do when Pie retires next month?"

Don answered for both of us. "Wait to see how we like his replacement. We'll either stay or retire. We've both got enough time in."

Elaine smiled. "Pie may have a surprise for you. I'll let him tell it."

Connie said, "Elaine, do any of our laws and international agreements have a noticeable effect on the environment? My school system is thinking of installing an advanced placement module for seniors on The Politics of Climate Change and I don't want to just parrot the conventional wisdom." Connie was a deputy superintendent of the Montgomery County school system.

"Some laws and agreements have an effect, some don't," Elaine answered. "The Clean Air Act and its Amendments, for instance, were pretty much responsible for cleaning up Pittsburgh and Los Angeles. Despite opposition from both the left and the right, we adopted a scheme nicknamed 'Cap and Trade'. Instead of the government telling electricity generators just when and how to reduce their emissions, the program tells the entire industry when and how much to reduce pollution. It does this by establishing a firm, maximum "cap" on emissions. Electricity generators hold an "allowance" for each ton of pollution they emit. These allowances can be traded or sold freely. This rewards companies that discover better ways to reduce emissions by allowing them to sell unneeded allowances in the market. Companies that can't reduce emissions can buy additional allowances from companies that don't need them, without undermining air quality. It's a market-based scheme that keeps the government off industry's back. As the Administration's token Republican, I'm proud of that."

Connie donned her trademarked "dumb broad" face. I looked at Don. Don looked at Alex. Alex looked at me. A collective "Uh, oh."

"So you think," asked Connie, "that the government should stay off people's backs?"

"Damn straight," said Elaine.

"Then how come so many Republicans want to pass laws banning abortions?"

Elaine stared at Connie, then burst out laughing. "Boy, I walked right into that, didn't I?"

"Yep," said Connie.

At which point Pie entered with a tray of hors d'oeuvres.

"Saved," said Elaine.

Pie put the tray down on the coffee table and Bessie joined us. "Dinner will be ready in about five minutes."

The hors d'oeuvres were little cherry tomatoes stuffed with tobiko roe and topped with something white. Bessie triumphed again – they were delicious.

"What's the white stuff on top?" Elaine asked.

"Egg white," Bessie answered. Then realized who she was talking to. "Chopped hard boiled egg white," she amended.

"So *nu*," Pie said to Alex, "How are you and your crew coping with the furlough?"

"I had everyone called," Alex responded, "and warned not to think. Thinking could cost them $5,000 and two years in the clink."

"Thinking could cost them?" Connie asked.

"That's right," Alex answered. "That's how computer scientists work. The first thing they do is think." He pondered this. "I suppose there'll be a lot more babies born nine months from now."

"The penalty for working is $5,000 and two years?" Bessie asked. "You mean you'll get paid for doing nothing and put in jail if you work? Who concocted this cockamamie system?"

"It started with the Founders," Don answered. "Article one Section nine of the Constitution says we can't work if the government doesn't have the money. Then President Grant's administration passed the Antideficiency Act."

"I think Grant drank a lot," I added.

"So who enforces this nonsense?" Connie asked.

Elaine laughed. "The Attorneys General. But since they're

'nonessential' personnel, they'll be subject to the penalties if they do their job."

Bessie stood up. "I think I'd better serve dinner. You know how to find the dining room. Sit down wherever you please."

She and Pie went to the kitchen and we followed orders.

The menu consisted of Wedding Chicken of Crete, crisp green beans and a butter lettuce salad with egg yolk dressing. Bessie cooked the chicken in an Etruscan-style clay pot. That method does wonderful things to a bird. As usual, Pie baked the bread. The wine was a nifty Sauvignon blanc from New Zealand.

Silence reigned while we immersed ourselves in the flavors. Finally, Connie came up for air.

"So besides the Clean Air Act, what other legislation or agreements have affected the environment?"

"Before we go into that," I said, "let me put this in context. Without the context the module might not make sense to the kids.

"In 1988, the UN and the World Meteorological Organization established The Intergovernmental Panel on Climate Change to provide the world with scientific reports on the state of knowledge in climate change and its potential impacts. Scientists from all over the world contribute to these reports. The first report was issued in 1990 and the latest report, the fifth, is upon us. Each report resolved a few more uncertainties and each report was more dire than the last. Those reports led the world to try to come to agreements on how to handle what was happening.

"I think the first report caused our DoTI-DRA committee to be formed."

Elaine nodded agreement.

Don said, "Okay, now that we've got the context, let me continue the narrative.

"By 1993, Clinton was in and he proposed a BTU tax. Essentially that was a carbon tax. It was supposed to encourage energy efficiency. But in 1994 the Gingrich Congress came in and not only did they kill that idea but the damn fools tried to repeal the Amendments to the Clean Air Act."

Elaine cut in. "They tried it despite the fact that the Amendments were a GOP invention! Why is it that every time my party does something brilliant a bunch of right wingnuts tries to screw it up?"

Connie opened her mouth. But before she could say anything, Elaine informed her that the question was rhetorical. Both of them subsided.

"So how come they *didn't* repeal them?" Bessie asked.

Don chuckled. "The regulated industries told them to piss off. When Cap and Trade was first proposed, the industries fought it. But it didn't take long before they realized that the additional effort to reduce their pollution didn't cost them all that much. And then they could sell their pollution permits, which gave them a really valuable portfolio. There's no question but that market-based pollution disincentives work. We should try it more often."

Pie added, "Understand that at the time, acid rain – which was caused by this type of pollution – was considered at least as big a problem as climate change. It's now a minor local or maybe regional problem."

"Okay," said Connie. "The Clean Air Act goes into the module. Then what?"

I said, "Before we get to 'then what', I think we should go back before the Clean Air Act to 1987 and the Montreal Protocol. That may be the most successful of all the international treaties. Even Ronald Reagan – the guy who removed the solar panels from the roof of the White House – called it a 'monumental achievement'."

"What did it do?"

Bessie said, "It dealt with the hole in the ozone. The hole was caused, for the most part by freon, which contains chlorofluorocarbons. These are gases that are released into the atmosphere by such things as fire extinguishers, aerosol cans, air conditioners, refrigerator coolants, and so on. Those products release the chlorofluorocarbons into the atmosphere, where they deplete the ozone layer. Now, the ozone layer protects the earth from the sun's ultra violet rays, and that causes health problems such as skin cancer, cataracts, and immune suppression. Most people recognized that something had to be done. Although I recall that Reagan's Secretary of the Interior," turning to Elaine, "What was his name?"

Elaine grimaced, "A name that shall live in infamy. James Watt."

"Yeah, James Watt. He didn't understand why people couldn't just wear hats and sunglasses."

I resumed the tale. "So the purpose of the Montreal Protocol was to get rid of the chlorofluorocarbons. Only a few countries didn't sign on – among them Afghanistan and Iraq – and those guys had other things to worry about. Anyway, the participation is nearly universal and includes the largest and richest nations. That's one requirement for a successful international treaty.

"Then, the agreement has an enforcement mechanism, which most international agreements don't have. The penalties for non-compliance include trade sanctions against products containing, or made by using chlorofluorocarbons. An enforcement mechanism is another requirement for a successful treaty.

"Plus, the cost of compliance is relatively low compared to the benefits. Complying is not going to cripple a country's economy.

"And finally, the treaty includes a fund to help the poorer countries switch from whatever they are using to chlorofluorocarbon-free technologies.

"So what's the result of all this? The hole in the ozone is closing. Best estimates are that it will be completely closed within the next couple of decades, although some stray chlorofluorocarbons may still be floating around in the atmosphere until mid-century."

"Wow," Connie said, "That was some treaty."

"Yeah," I finished, "but not the end of the story. It turns out that some of the alternatives to chlorofluorocarbons contribute to the greenhouse effect. We haven't yet found a universal alternative that mimics freon, but we've got packages of alternatives and my guess is that sooner, rather than later, a universal alternative will be found."

Pie stood up. "Let's go into the living room for coffee and dessert and finish the discussion."

We guests arranged ourselves around the big coffee table while Pie and Bessie fetched the coffee pot and a large tray of fruit and cheese.

Connie said, "Mmphblfrrrrpb."

A chorus of "What did you say?"

Connie washed down the last of her cracker. "Then what happened?"

Pie responded. *"Mishegoss!* The brightest minds in the universe assembled in Kyoto, Japan with the intention of duplicating the success of the Montreal Protocol, only this time they would tackle greenhouse gases. So what did they do?

"Well, let's look at what made Montreal a success. Getting rid of chlorofluorocarbons wasn't very costly compared to the benefits everyone got. That isn't the case with greenhouse gases. At least in the short run, shifting from domestic fossil fuels to some undefined substitute would cost a lot of money."

"Why?" Connie asked.

"Because coal plants are both the cheapest way to generate energy and the worst pollutants. If we raise the cost of manufacturing things we won't manufacture as much. And if we don't manufacture as much we'll lose revenue and jobs. Best estimate is five million jobs."

"But that's the short run," Connie said. "In the long run both we and the rest of the world will be much better off."

"Yeah," Elaine put in. "But as they say, 'In the long run we'll all be dead.'"

Alex woke up. "Hey guys, fascinating as it is, the question isn't about the merits of coal versus something else, but why the Kyoto Protocol failed. It looks like a major reason is that the US decided that to comply with the targets would cost too much.

"And if we decided not to participate, then one of the big reasons for the success of Montreal – participation by the big, rich countries – didn't happen with Kyoto."

Connie looked decidedly unhappy. "So you're saying that the treaty failed mostly because the US didn't like it and wouldn't adopt it."

Don looked fondly at his wife. "Don't bet on that, hon. Canada accepted her target for emissions reduction of six percent below 1990 levels by 2012. By 2008 her greenhouse gas emissions had risen by about twenty four percent. She withdrew from the Protocol before they could slap a fine on her. In about the same time period, *our* emissions rose about ten percent. Not good, but not as bad as Canada – a country that did sign the treaty.

"Our not signing didn't really matter, Con. These are sovereign nations. And a sovereign nation is gonna do what a sovereign nation is gonna do. If they don't see it as in their best interest they're not gonna do it, whether they sign the thing or not."

Elaine added, "Participation and cost weren't the only things. There was the little matter of unequal enforcement. They divided the world into developed and developing nations. All countries get tradeable credits for reducing emissions – similar to our Clean Air Act. But only developed countries get targets for reducing emissions and fined for missing the targets. But in their clueless state the drafters didn't recognize how fast some of the "developing" countries – China, India, Brazil, for instance -- were going to develop. So what we have now is that China is getting credits for their photovoltaic industry and nothing bad happens to them as they put one hundred coal plants on line each week. About twelve hundred coal plants are planned worldwide, about three quarters of them in China and India."

Connie's mouth dropped. "Are you saying that China is firing up a hundred of those plants a week and nothing bad is happening to it?"

"Oh," I said, "something bad *will* happen to it. Coal burners use a humongous amount of water and the areas where China is putting them don't have all that much water. Question is how much money they're going to save when they have to factor in hauling water to those places.

"I've heard a number of schemes for getting water there when they run out. I particularly like the one that postulates towing glaciers from the Poles. I'm curious to see how that's going to happen as the glaciers continue to melt."

"But why did the Kyoto Protocol include a carrot and no stick for those countries?"

"It was a way to pave the road to hell," Elaine explained. "The industrial revolution was what caused all of the emission problems. The breaks given to the developing countries were thought to be a way to allow them to skip the bad effects of the industrial revolution while still permitting them to develop.

"At any rate, there was no way we were going to sign it." Elaine thought for a minute. "That's not quite accurate. Clinton did sign it. But before it ever got to the Senate for ratification, that body unanimously passed the Byrd-Hagel Resolution which made it clear that the Senate was not going to ratify anything that tied us to a legally binding emissions reduction target. The Kyoto Protocol would have done just that – tied us to a reduction target of thirty to thirty five percent. No government could have made that promise. So the Protocol wasn't submitted to the Senate for ratification."

I stuck another two cents in. "I take it that you know about the Virginia governor slapping a tax on hybrid cars because they don't buy as much fuel as gas guzzlers. Well, a similar clause went into the Kyoto Protocol. The OPEC states got compensation because other nations would buy less oil. As far as the Senate was concerned, Kyoto was as attractive as a rancid sausage."

"So," said Connie, "the Kyoto Protocol was a failure."

"I would say so," Pie said. "It was up for renewal in 2012 and besides us and Australia, the original non-signers, Canada, Japan, New

Zealand, and Russia haven't signed on for the second round. That doesn't sound like a success to me.

"But some people think that it had a beneficial effect in that it spurred a lot of innovations that reduce emissions."

"Like what?" Don asked.

Pie shrugged. "There's been some successful efforts to capture anesthetic gasses and preventing them from entering the atmosphere. About twenty hospitals in Ontario are using the technology. And there have been some test sites taking CO_2, liquefying it and putting it in underground caverns.

"Plus a lot of money has gone into photovoltaics, concentrated solar power, and so on. Nothing really dramatic."

"And all this research came about because of Kyoto?" Don asked. "Come on, Pie, this research pre-dates Kyoto by decades."

Pie laughed. "I'm just reciting the green mantra. I didn't say I believed it."

Don continued, "There are ways to curb global warming without crippling civilization. The partial switch from coal to gas for electricity production alone, a switch that the despised fracking technology made possible, has done more to slow US greenhouse gas emissions than all of the green technologies combined."

"But Don," Connie protested, "fracking causes all sorts of other environmental problems."

"Hon, nuthin' costs nuthin'. We have to decide what our priorities are."

"Don't 'hon' me, buster. One of the biggest problems with fracking is the emission of methane, which is more harmful to the environment than carbon dioxide. Plus the problems of contaminated water and God knows what else. We can't decide our priorities until we know what side effects we're breeding. You may recall that we're closing the ozone layer at the expense of increasing greenhouse gases."

"Okay," Bessie interceded. "you two duke it out on the way home. Meanwhile, what's happening post-Kyoto?"

"Well, we kind of milled around for several years," Elaine answered. "Bush and Cheney both had significant ties to the fossil fuel industry and besides that they weren't exactly enamored with the UN and multinational treaties, so we were essentially out of the international climate policy game. On top of that, 911 happened, our economy weakened, and competition with China was getting scarier, so there wasn't much domestic activity going on either. Bea's committee and a few others like it were just about it.

"Then Al Gore came out with *An Inconvenient Truth* in 2006 and public discussion of climate change burgeoned. It's hard to overestimate the effect that the film had on the American public. Aside from all of the presentations that Al made – he says he gave over a thousand of them – the film got two Academy Awards, for a documentary and for the music. Melissa Etheridge sang 'I Need to Wake Up'. You can still catch it on YouTube. Then Al got a Nobel Prize. Not bad going for a failed presidential candidate. Al deserved the Nobel.

"But still, the climate change denial machine chugs on. They jumped on the errors in *An Inconvenient Truth* and there's no denying that there are errors. But nonetheless the basic inconvenient truth is that we're in trouble. And unless we do something damn quick, our descendants, if we continue to have any, are going to be fried, frozen, drowned, blown away, or otherwise severely damaged."

Pie weighed in. "Those nincompoops pointed out that the

extremely hot years from 1998 through 2000, followed by the only *very* hot years from 2000 to 2007 'prove' that there is no such thing as climate change. I don't know if they're stupid, uneducated, willfully obtuse, or just run-of-the-mill economists. No real scientist would ever cherry-pick data from long-term trends."

Bessie laughed. "Pie was bitten by an economist when he was a kid and he's been afraid of them ever since."

Pie gave her a friendly smack on top of her head.

"That's not helping my module," Connie grumped. "Did anything besides Al Gore happen after Kyoto?"

"Sure," Don said. "Copenhagen happened in 2009. That had to be the nuttiest Conference ever. Over fifteen thousand negotiators and activists converged on a venue that holds just few thousand. So most of those folk spent their time in the many Copenhagen bars while the favored few negotiated. China and India took a hard line against any commitments and there was brouhaha-ing all around. At one point, Obama and Hillary Clinton, 'allegedly' uninvited, joined a meeting of the Chinese, Indian and Brazilian leaders. Obama said he didn't want them negotiating in secret.

"Whether or not they crashed the party, a sort of deal came out of it. It provided a system for monitoring and reporting progress toward pollution reduction goals, for hundreds of billions of dollars to go from the rich countries to the countries really vulnerable to climate change, and a goal of limiting total global temperature rise to no more than two degrees.

"It wasn't really a binding accord, but it set the stage for the next meeting, in Cancun, Mexico in 2010."

Elaine continued the story. "Cancun is a real breakthrough. It's the first time that we, China, and all of the other major greenhouse gas emitters set their national pollution targets into a formal UN agreement."

"How did that happen?" Connie asked.

"Because it was a bottom-up agreement. Instead of a voice from above dictating the targets, each country stipulated what it was willing to do and that's what was written into the agreement. That gives some hope that they'll stick to their promises.

"The bottom-up approach also lets the developing countries carve out places that are most important to them and concentrate their efforts there. The UN Reducing Emissions from Deforestation and Degradation program is a good example. Indonesia has one of the most significant areas of largely-intact tropical forest in the world, but it's under threat. With the Cancun Agreement, they can focus on their forests without worrying about other areas that have little meaning for them. A similar, but broader program, Nationally Appropriate Mitigation Actions, can be tailored to the major causes of pollution in each developing country and they aren't forced to act in sectors that have nothing much to do with them.

"Even the developed countries' commitments can be tailored somewhat. Canada, for instance, put in contingencies to its target excluding things like uncontrolled wildfires which are beyond that their control.

"The bottom-up approach is working."

"Sure," Connie said. "But it's not going to get us where we need to go."

"Nope," said Elaine. "But it'll get us closer than any other method we've tried. No known method is going to undo the damage the last couple of centuries have done to the environment. But the closer we edge toward containing the damage the easier the next round of agreements will be. What we've found out is that the perfect is the enemy of the good.

"One hundred and ninety three nations were there to agree on the Accord and the only dissenter was Bolivia."

"Bolivia?" Alex yelped. "Why Bolivia?"

"Ostensibly, they wanted the perfection of top-down pollution targets."

"Ostensibly? What was the real reason?"

Elaine laughed. "They wanted to give the U.S. one in the eye. If we had voted 'nay' they'd have voted 'yea'

"The major tangible accomplishment of Cancun, aside from moving to bottom-up targets, was the finance package which has been a bone of contention since forever.

"A Green Climate Fund will be the mechanism to deliver support for truly urgent climate actions like reducing emissions through protecting forests, and shifting to greener energy technologies. The fund will also deliver resources to newly established technology centers which will oversee research, scientific exchange and technical support for countries looking to improve efficiency and reduce emissions from sectors like energy production, transportation, and buildings.

"Then there was the question of transparency of finance. This was one of many issues on which the chairperson, Mexico's Patricia Espinosa, showed extraordinary diplomatic skills. Developing countries had been advocating for a process to ensure that the delivery of climate finance would be transparent and there would be a system to monitor and verify the promised funds. The final agreement included a new registry to record developing country efforts to reduce emissions and to match those actions to finance and technical support.

"And finally, the Agreement formalized the Copenhagen commitments to deliver $30 billion through 2012. Long term funding was put off for another Conference."

"You said 'tangible' accomplishment, was there an intangible accomplishment?" Connie asked.

"Absolutely. This agreement did more to build the spirit of compromise needed for countries to work together on all global challenges than anything that has ever gone before. I talked to some of our negotiators and they said they'd never experienced anything like it. Sworn enemies were working together, laughing together, dining together, and drinking together –at least those who weren't Muslim were drinking. It would be ironic if the climate changes that are tearing the Earth apart were to bring its people together."

"And that's it?" said Connie.

"Just about," Pie answered. "There have been other meetings and conferences – the one in Durban, for instance – but for the most part they've been building on Cancun.

"Not that we can expect a clear highway to greenhouse gas elimination. There are still some issues dividing the haves and have-nots, and I'll be surprised if Japan doesn't pull out. Between earthquake and tsunami, the country's nuclear reactors were compromised and they have to resort to importing fossil fuels. But still, we're edging closer to reducing the greenhouse gasses.

"Unfortunately, this last report of the International Panel is enough to dampen optimism. First and not surprising, it said that global warming is for real. No more uncertainties. Second, scientists are sure that humans are driving global warming. Third, carbon dioxide is higher than it has been in a million years. Fourth, that whatever the cherry-pickers may claim, the long term trend is going up. There's been a temporary slowdown due to a number of factors including a short term decline in solar radiation reaching the earth because of volcanic eruptions, but the trend is still up. Fifth, projections of sea level rise have increased. Sea levels could rise by more than three feet. And finally, a lot of the global warming is irreversible and will continue for centuries."

We sat around for a while looking glum.

I finally asked, "Pie, Elaine said you had a surprise for us."

Pie grinned. "Indeed. The President has asked me to be the next Secretary of DoTI. I said I'd do it if I could name my successor at LIT."

"And what did the White House say about that?"

"Well," said Elaine, "as far as LIT is concerned, I'm the White House and I said okay."

"And what does Bessie say about that?"

"Bessie says," said Bessie, "'Wonderful'. The University of Maryland offered me a Distinguished Professorship and since Pie will be staying in the area, I can accept without guilt."

"So who's your successor going to be?" Don asked Pie.

"Well," said Pie, "my first choice was Jason Fromlich, but he's in the middle of some important research and he can't leave it now. He may be willing to be the Director when the new appointee leaves."

"And who might that be?"

"You or Don."

"Whoa," said Don. I'm a budget guy. The perfect deputy. No way would I make a good Director. But I'll stay if Bea takes it."

"Cut it out," I said. "You need a scientist in that position and a management scientist is an oxymoron."

"You don't need a scientist as Director," Pie said. "You just need a scientist in the Director's office. Molly Cameron is about to retire. She may be willing to stay on in that position or, if not, at least get someone suitable. I don't want to destroy the chemistry that we've built up over the last couple of decades."

"Still..." I began, when Alex started to laugh.

"What's so funny," Bessie asked.

When he stopped laughing Alex said, "After twenty years Lenore finally got used to a senior manager and a Center Director canoodling in the parking lot. It'd take her another twenty years to get used to the *Director* canoodling with a Center Director." He started laughing again.

Then Don and Connie started to laugh.

Then I started to laugh.

"Okay," I said to Pie. "I'll do it."